D0381133

Presents~

What do you love most about reading Harlequin Presents books? From what you tell us, it's our sexy foreign heroes, exciting and emotionally intense relationships, generous helpings of pure passion and glamorous international settings that bring you pleasure!

Welcome to February 2007's stunning selection of eight novels that bring you emotion, passion and excitement galore, as you are whisked around the world to meet men who make love in many languages. And you'll also find your favorite authors: Penny Jordan, Lucy Monroe, Kate Walker, Susan Stephens, Sandra Field, Carole Mortimer, Elizabeth Power and Anne McAllister.

Sit back and let us entertain you....

*Legally wed,
but he's never said,
"I love you."
They're...*

*The series where marriages are made
in haste...and love comes later.*

*Look out for more WEDLOCKED!
wedding stories available only from
Harlequin Presents®*

In March:
The Kouvaris Marriage
by Diana Hamilton
#2614

Sandra Field

THE MILLIONAIRE'S PREGNANT WIFE

TORONTO • NEW YORK • LONDON
AMSTERDAM • PARIS • SYDNEY • HAMBURG
STOCKHOLM • ATHENS • TOKYO • MILAN • MADRID
PRAGUE • WARSAW • BUDAPEST • AUCKLAND

ISBN-13: 978-0-373-12607-1
ISBN-10:   0-373-12607-7

THE MILLIONAIRE'S PREGNANT WIFE

First North American Publication 2007.

Copyright © 2006 by Sandra Field.

www.eHarlequin.com

Printed in U.S.A.

All about the author...
Sandra Field

Although born in England, **SANDRA FIELD** has lived most of her life in Canada; she says the silence and emptiness of the north speak to her particularly. While she enjoys traveling and passing on her sense of a new place, she often chooses to write about the city that is now her home. She's been very fortunate for years to be able to combine a love of travel (particularly to the north—she doesn't do heat well) with her writing, by describing settings that most people will probably never visit.

Kayaking and canoeing, hiking and gardening, listening to music and reading are all sources of great pleasure. But best of all are good friends— some going back to high school days—and her family. She has a beautiful daughter-in-law and the two most delightful, handsome and intelligent grandchildren in the world (of course!).

Sandra has always loved to read, fascinated by the lure of being drawn into the other world of the story. And her first book was published as *To Trust My Love*. Sandra says, "I write out of my experience. I have learned that love with its joys and its pains is all-important. I hope this knowledge enriches my writing, and touches a chord in you, the reader."

CHAPTER ONE

IF HE HAD to deal with inheriting a mansion he'd hated on sight, he'd rather do it alone.

If he had to go through all the boxes in one room of that mansion, searching for clues to a mother about whom—to put it mildly—he felt ambivalent, he'd much rather do it alone. But it would take forever, and Luke Griffin didn't have forever. He had a financial empire to maintain.

He needed help.

Not his usual way of operating. He'd been doing things on his own since he was too little to remember.

He thumbed through the *Yellow Pages* again until he found the company that had looked like a helpful lead. Organize Your Home. With a name like that, surely someone should be able to help him go through the boxes? The other choice was to haul them to the dump.

They were his only chance to find out anything about his past. Luke punched the numbers and waited for the ring.

"Hello?"

A woman's voice. A rich contralto voice, with an under-tone of huskiness that managed to turn two ordinary syllables into something very close to an invitation. He said briskly, "Is this Organize Your Home?"

"You have the right number," the woman said. "But the business is no longer in operation...sorry."

She didn't sound sorry. She sounded jubilant, like sunlight through the amber depths of brandy. "My name's Luke Griffin," he said. "I'm staying temporarily at Griffin's Keep, and I have at least three days' work for you."

"I'm sorry, Mr. Griffin—as I said, I've disbanded the company. Last week."

He said implacably, "What do you usually charge per hour?"

"That's not—"

"Just answer the question. And perhaps you could tell me your name?"

Her voice warmed with temper. "Kelsey North. Forty dollars an hour. It's not on."

"I'll pay two hundred and fifty an hour. Multiply that by three days—I'm sure you can do the math."

There was a taut silence. Then she said crisply, "What sort of work?"

"My grandmother—Sylvia Griffin—left me some papers that are of personal interest. Unfortunately they're scattered throughout her financial records. Boxes and boxes of them, and each one has to be gone through page by page. I'm a busy man and I have to get back to Manhattan. I can't take the time to do this on my own."

"I see," Kelsey North said. "Give me your number. I'll call you back later this evening."

He rhymed off the numbers on the phone. "I look forward to hearing from you," he said smoothly. "Goodbye, Ms North."

The woman at the other end banged the receiver down with a force that was not remotely professional. If she was one of his employees, she'd be taking a course on customer relations, Luke thought, idly wondering why she'd closed her business. Although with a voice like that she was wasted organizing other people's closets.

If, when she called back, she said no, he was in deep trouble.

He'd up the rate to five hundred an hour. That'd get her, he thought cynically, and went to see if he could rustle up a cup of coffee in the archaic kitchen of Griffin's Keep.

KELSEY GLARED AT the receiver as if Luke Griffin was standing on top of it. The nerve of the man. The arrogance. As if she was supposed to levitate six feet in the air the moment he said jump.

Organize Your Home no longer existed. Finished. *Kaput.* She was free, free, free!

She did an impromptu twirl around the living room, then sat down again at the table where she'd been working on her list when the phone had rung. It was a list, in bright red marker, of all the things she wanted to do now that her life was her own.

Go to art school. Travel. Paint a masterpiece. Paint her toenails purple. Have torrid sex.

Her brow knitted. She crossed out *torrid.* Any kind of sex would do, wouldn't it? Still frowning, she erased *Have sex* and substituted *Have an affair.* It sounded more romantic. Classier. Especially if she had it with someone tall, dark and handsome, who'd treat her like a piece of breakable china and give her roses and breakfast in bed.

None of her dates in the last few years had been tall, dark and handsome; there wasn't much choice in Hadley, the village where she lived. Kelsey heaved a sigh, then added *Holiday* to her list.

But until she sold the house, how could she afford a holiday? Nearly all her savings had gone to the art school in Manhattan as the deposit with her application.

Two hundred and fifty dollars an hour for three days. Six thousand dollars.

Yes, she could do the math.

He was bribing her, she thought with a spurt of rage. The famous—or rather, infamous—Luke Griffin thought she could be bought.

Well, she could. Couldn't she?

Why did everything always have to come down to money?

If she had six thousand dollars she could pay for her first two semesters and have a bit left for a trip. Somewhere south, where it was warm.

It wasn't as though Luke Griffin couldn't afford it. He could. He'd graduated from millions to billions several years ago, or so Alice at the post office said.

Organizing a dead woman's papers wasn't anywhere on her list.

So what? She'd go to Griffin's Keep, work her butt off for three days, take the money and run. And in the meantime she'd check the internet for inexpensive package tours to a tropical island with palm trees, white sand and drinks with little colored umbrellas in them. Quickly, before she could change her mind, Kelsey picked up the phone and dialed the number for Griffin's Keep.

Luke brushed a layer of dust off the receiver and held it to his ear. "Luke Griffin."

"This is Kelsey North. What time do you want me to start?"

Her brandy-smooth voice was overlaid with irritation. "Tomorrow morning at eight-thirty," he said. "I can't find anything but mouse droppings in the pantry, so if you need caffeine to get yourself moving in the morning, you'd better bring your own." He smiled into the phone. "Wear old clothes, the place hasn't been cleaned in months. I look forward to meeting you, Ms North." Gently he put the phone down.

One more woman who could be bought, he thought, and wondered if her appearance would in any way measure up to the beauty of her voice.

* * *

KELSEY DRESSED WITH care the next morning. Then she picked up a can of Colombian blend and a carton of coffee cream, and left the house. Her car started like a dream, and the ten-minute drive to Griffin's Keep gave her time to think.

Since Sylvia Griffin's death a few days ago, gossip had run rife in Hadley. Sylvia's grandson, whose name was Luke, hadn't gotten a cent in her will; he'd inherited the whole packet; he was bringing his stretch limo to her funeral; he was in Hong Kong and would arrive by helicopter; he was worth one billion dollars, ten billion, a hundred billion...

There was consensus on only one subject: women fell like flies at his approach, and his mistresses were legendary for their beauty, wealth and elegance.

In the end, he hadn't bothered attending his grandmother's funeral at all, Kelsey mused, driving down a side road where last week's snow still lingered in the ditches. He'd arrived late yesterday, the day after the funeral. As far as she knew, he'd never taken the time to visit Sylvia while she was alive, and certainly not in her last brief illness. Too busy amassing his fortune and bedding every beauty in sight, she thought unkindly, and pulled into the driveway of Griffin's Keep.

Her heart beating a little faster than usual, Kelsey rang the doorbell. The brass around it was pitted and tarnished.

Through the narrow windows on either side of the door she heard the thud of footsteps on the stairs, then the door was yanked open. Her jaw dropped.

Luke Griffin was wearing jeans with the button undone, and a thin white T-shirt that molded every muscle in his chest. There was an awful lot of muscle, she thought, swallowing, and forced her gaze upward. A long way up. Tall. Yep, he was tall, all right. His hair, ruffled and untidy, was dark as night; dark stubble shadowed his cheeks and jawline.

So was he handsome? His eyes, deepset, were of a startling blue under brows as dark as his hair; his lashes were like dabs of soot. Add a decided nose, jutting cheekbones and a strongly carved mouth that made her feel weak just to look at it, and she was left with a face infused with character, none of it gentle. Forceful, decisive, ruthless: the words tumbled through her brain. Handsome, she thought faintly, had been left way behind.

"Luke Griffin," he said, running long, lean fingers through his disordered hair and stifling a yawn. "Sorry, I only just woke up. Jet-lagged the wrong way—this feels like three in the morning."

"You told me to arrive at eight-thirty," she said edgily.

"Yeah." His smile shot through her like a sunburst. "Just goes to show what lousy decisions I make when I cross the dateline. Come on in, and I'll show you what I want done." His eyes fell to the package she was carrying. "Don't tell me that's coffee? Real coffee?"

"Colombian."

"You're a jewel among women," he said fervently, and pulled her into the house, shutting the door behind her.

Because his fingers were gripping her elbow, she was entirely too close to that tautly muscled chest. He smelled warm and indescribably male: a man who'd just climbed out of bed.

Bed, Kelsey thought faintly. Torrid sex.

"Is something wrong?" he said.

"No! Of course not." Maybe he slept naked.

He gave her another of those brain-sizzling smiles. "I know you're here to sort papers. But if you could produce a decent mug of coffee in that horror of a kitchen, I'd be everlastingly grateful."

Charm. Hadn't gossip—indirectly—warned her he could charm the birds out of the trees? Or, to be more accurate, charm a woman who'd been determined to dislike him? "I'll try," she said.

"I'll go have a shower. I promise I'll be fully awake when I come downstairs, Ms North."

"Kelsey. I prefer to be called Kelsey."

"Luke, then." He nodded to his left. "The boxes are in the third room down the hall."

"Okay."

Okay? Was that all she could come up with? Her mouth dry, she watched him take the stairs—a curving sweep of mahogany—two by two. His bare feet left tracks in the thick dust.

The kitchen. Coffee. Focus, Kelsey.

How would she last three days without jumping him? She, who'd never jumped a man in her life.

Blindly she marched down the hall until she located the kitchen, with its outmoded appliances and stale-smelling grease over counters and floor. For a moment Kelsey forgot about Luke Griffin, stabbed with pity that someone who'd been a very rich woman could have lived in such squalor.

If Luke had taken the time to visit he could have hired a housekeeper, Kelsey thought, finding a battered percolator in a cupboard and scrubbing it in the filthy sink. How could he have ignored his grandmother so woefully while she was alive, yet be so intent on going through her papers now that she was dead?

It was unforgivable.

Holding tight to her anger, Kelsey put the coffee on, then located the room with the boxes.

Piles of boxes, shutting out the light from the narrow window, leaning drunkenly against the wallpaper. It would take hours and hours to go through them. Was Luke Griffin out of his mind?

Biting her lip, Kelsey headed back to the kitchen and washed two mugs.

LUKE FASTENED HIS jeans and pulled a dark blue sweater over his head. Socks. He needed socks. He rummaged through his suitcase, wishing he could adjust to eastern time and feel even minimally awake.

Kelsey North didn't in any way match her sexy voice.

Homely as a board fence.

Seizing a pair of black socks, he sat down on the bed to pull them on. Her tweed suit, too large and in a depressing shade of mud-brown, had a boxy jacket and a loose-cut long skirt; her shirt was man-tailored, no-nonsense white cotton, buttoned high to her throat, and she was wearing horn-rimmed glasses. Her shoes were clunky brown lace-ups.

It was a mystery to him why a woman like her—a young woman, with a very sexy voice—would choose to make the worst of herself. Those awful glasses. That suit. She must have searched high and low to find something so ill-fitting. So hideous.

Even her lipstick was an unflattering shade of pale pink.

He dragged a comb through his hair. While her hair wasn't a bad color, sort of a reddish-brown, how could a man appreciate it when it was skewered to her scalp? Her ankles weren't bad, though.

He'd noticed every detail, he thought wryly. But hadn't he been hoping, subconsciously, that the rest of her would interest him as much as her voice? That she might relieve the tedium of three days stuck in a place he didn't want to be?

Not a hope.

Luke pulled on a pair of shoes, ran downstairs, then followed his nose to the kitchen. "Coffee," he said. "Will you marry me?"

Kelsey blinked. "You'd better taste it first."

"I don't need to. Name the date."

She said, with complete truth, "Marriage isn't on my list, Mr. Griffin."

"List? Ah, of course. Organize Your Home—you'd have to be a maker of lists. Are they arranged alphabetically?" He poured himself a mug of coffee, added a liberal dollop of cream and raised it to his lips. "You can file this under H for heaven."

"I'd file you under C for charm," she said, more tartly than she'd intended.

"Why do I think that's not a compliment?"

"Because it isn't. Charm's not to be trusted." She poured her own coffee. "I've opened a couple of the boxes. What exactly are you hoping to find?"

Taking his time, Luke looked her up and down, from the sagging hem of her skirt to the pencil stuck in her hair. "B for business...I get the message."

"At two hundred and fifty dollars an hour, that might be advisable."

"Your tongue doesn't match your outfit," he said. "You're clearly intelligent—so why do you dress like that?"

She flushed, and for the first time he noticed the delicate rise of her cheekbones under the thick rims of her glasses. She said tightly, "The way I dress is nothing to do with you."

"I don't require all the women in my life to be beautiful, or even pretty," he said thoughtfully. "But I do require character—the confidence, the flair to dress like a beautiful woman."

"*All* the women?" Kelsey repeated ironically. "I'm sure they mob you."

"Money's a powerful aphrodisiac."

"Money is why I'm here," she said crisply. "Would you please tell me what we're looking for in all those boxes?"

Luke wished he knew the answer to that question. It was a very obvious question, and one he should have anticipated. He took another big gulp of coffee, feeling it course down his throat. "My mother was Sylvia Griffin's daughter," he said curtly. "We're looking for anything at all relating to Rosemary Griffin. You're to put any papers bearing her name aside without reading them."

Kelsey's flush deepened. "There's no need to be insulting."

"I'm just stating the parameters of the job."

She should quit. Right now. But for six thousand dollars, surely she could swallow an insult or two? "Very well," she said, with rather overdone politeness. "If you'll excuse me, I'll get started."

As Luke watched her march out of the kitchen, he couldn't even tell if her hips were swinging under that extraordinarily unsexy skirt. Her ankles, however, were indeed very shapely.

With an impatient sigh he drained his mug, then refilled it. He should have thought this whole venture through. By calling Kelsey in to help, he'd invited a virtual stranger to look for papers relating to his mother. How was she going to earmark them without at least partially reading them?

He was known worldwide for his strong sense of privacy; it drove the media crazy. Yet he'd just directed a lippy woman to go through files whose contents could be highly personal.

Well done, Luke. Grimacing, he poured cream in his coffee and left the kitchen. Kelsey was already set up on a table by the window, the first box open, papers neatly piled on the table. Luke brought another table in from the parlor, and followed suit. For the space of three hours, they worked in silence.

Kelsey was the first to stop. She stood up, stretching the tension from her neck. Tension which had more to do with sitting ten feet from Luke Griffin all morning than her futile search. His focus had been formidable, his face grim, nothing in his demeanor encouraging conversation.

"I haven't found anything," she said. "What about you?"

"Inventories of furniture, stock certificates and a grocery list."

She looked over at the pile of boxes. "It's a huge job."

Luke wasn't enjoying searching through the details of Sylvia Griffin's life. Standing up, he said brusquely, "I'll double your pay."

Kelsey's chin jerked up. "You will not."

"When I make an offer like that, most people say *Thank you very much, Mr. Griffin.*"

"I'm not most people."

"I'll damn well pay you what I want."

"Fine. I'll donate the excess to a home for stray dogs. Or to a fund for elderly women who live alone and whose grandsons don't even bother to visit them."

He stepped closer, noticing with part of his brain how she stood her ground, even though panic was flaring in her eyes. "Until I got the message in Hong Kong three days ago that she'd died, I didn't even know I had a grandmother," he said, clipping off every word. "So don't lay guilt trips on me, Kelsey North—I won't wear 'em."

"You didn't know?" she repeated stupidly.

"Right."

For reasons she couldn't have articulated, Kelsey believed him instantly. "So that's why you never visited her...and you got the message too late to attend her funeral."

"On the day she was buried I was in the wilds of Cambodia."

"Why didn't your mother tell you about her?"

He winced; unerringly, Kelsey had asked the question that had been tormenting him for the last few days. He said evasively, "I can only assume my mother left this house before I was born. Don't tell me gossip hasn't been rampant in the village since Sylvia died—I'm sure you can fill in the details."

Kelsey said quietly, "All I've ever heard is that your mother left home when she was seventeen."

"Was she pregnant?" he flashed, the words out before he could censor them.

"People speculated that she was. But it was only speculation."

"Let's break for lunch," he grated. "Be back here in an hour."

His eyes were ice-blue, his mouth a tight line. Kelsey didn't dare ask if his mother was still alive; he looked like he'd take her head off if she as much as opened her mouth. She brushed past him, her brain whirling. Earlier, she'd cast him as the villain, but she'd been wrong. He'd been totally ignorant of his grandmother's existence.

Wouldn't Alice at the post office love to hear *that* juicy little morsel?

Too bad. She wasn't going to hear it from Kelsey.

Tomorrow she'd bring sandwiches, Kelsey decided, and work through lunch. And tonight she'd take a couple of boxes home with her and go through them there. The sooner this job was done the better. Luke Griffin didn't just spell H for handsome or S for sex. He spelled D for danger.

CHAPTER TWO

THE FOLLOWING DAY, as dusk fell, Luke and Kelsey carried a couple of boxes out to her car. Luke drew a deep breath of the chill, damp air. January at its worst, he thought, crunching through a patch of unmelted snow, catching a glimpse of a pale moon through wind-torn clouds. Carefully balancing the box on the rear bumper, he opened the trunk, waited for Kelsey to dump her box in, then added his own. He slammed the trunk shut and opened her car door.

"Thank you," she said stiffly, and climbed in.

As she banged snow from her shoes, her skirt inadvertently rode up her legs. Admirable legs, he thought with sudden sharp interest, watching as she hastily hitched the thick tweed back in place. Her wrist, under the cuff of her jacket, was slender, the skin smooth. And it wasn't the first time he'd seen a flush mount her cheekbones, which were also admirable.

He toyed with the very strong temptation to yank the glasses off her nose. Keeping his hands firmly at his sides, he said, "See you tomorrow."

She mumbled something under her breath, thrust the key in the lock, clashed the gears and drove away. It was time he headed back to the city if he was having sexual fantasies about the frumpy Ms North, Luke thought caustically

Maybe he should ship the boxes to his penthouse and go

through them at his leisure. If he was in Manhattan he could be having dinner at Cisco's, with someone like Clarisse or Lindsay.

Neither of them had a temper. Unlike Kelsey. No, Clarisse and Lindsay wouldn't risk ruffling his billion-dollar feathers.

He walked slowly up the front steps. A headache was banding his forehead. So far, Kelsey had found Rosemary Griffin's birth certificate, and he'd found the bill from the exclusive clinic where his mother had been born. And that was it.

He'd learned one other thing. Kelsey might top America's Worst-Dressed List, but she sure knew how to work. Thorough, uncomplaining and dedicated: if he'd been writing a reference for her, he'd have used all three words.

He could have added unforthcoming. The only fact he knew about her was that she'd lived all her life in Hadley. He'd found that out by asking.

He himself was in no mood for idle conversation. Why, then, did it irritate the hell out of him that she'd discouraged anything resembling personal chitchat?

Luke walked slowly up the front steps and forced himself to go through one more box. The wind was moaning in the gutters and rattling a loose shingle; suddenly he couldn't stand being alone for one more minute in his grandmother's house, a house as withholding of its secrets as its dead owner.

He ran upstairs, changed into a clean sweater and jeans, and picked up his car keys.

THREE-QUARTERS OF an hour later, Luke got out of his car, carrying a thick brown paper bag. Kelsey's little house was set in a grove of old lilac bushes and tall yews; lights blazed in nearly every room. He climbed her front steps and rang the bell.

Janis Joplin was emoting at the top of her lungs. Luke rang the bell again, then turned the handle and found the door unlocked. The song came to an end as he pushed on the door and walked in. The hinges squealed like an animal in pain.

A woman came running down the stairs. When she saw him, she stopped dead on the fourth step down. Her hair was a tumbled mass of chestnut curls, framing eyes of a rich, velvety brown. She was slender-waisted, slim-hipped, with legs that seemed to go on forever.

Her low-necked orange shirt clung to her breasts; her jeans were skin-tight. Her toenails, he noticed blankly, were painted purple.

Her mouth… He gaped at it. Her lips, too, were orange, a glossy lipstick smoothed over their soft, voluptuous curves.

Lust coursed through his veins. He said awkwardly, "Oh…I was looking for Kelsey North. But I must have got the wrong address. Sorry to have bothered you…"

"Very funny," the woman said, in a husky contralto voice. *"Kelsey?"*

"Who did you think it was?"

"I—er, you've changed your clothes," he said. With a distant part of his brain he wondered what had happened to the Luke Griffin who'd dated famous beauties from Manhattan to Milan, and who was unfailingly suave.

Descending the last of the stairs and putting her hands on her hips, she said coldly, "I don't want any more boxes, and if you've lost your way I can direct you wherever you want to go."

She smelled delicious. The other Kelsey, the brown tweed Kelsey, smelled of worthy soap. Swallowing hard, Luke said, "Have you eaten dinner?"

"No. I've been going through the boxes I brought home."

"Good." He indicated the bag in his hands. "I brought it with me. From the bistro ten miles down the road." The bistro on the rich side of the peninsula, he thought, the same side as Griffin's Keep. Hadley, seven miles away, might as well be on another planet.

"You brought dinner with you? To eat here?"

"Yes." He gave her a winning smile. "I couldn't stand one more evening alone in that house."

Kelsey said carefully, "Am I missing something? I may only be from Hadley, but I thought it was customary to *ask* a woman if she wanted to have dinner with you."

"If I'd phoned, would you have said yes?"

"No, of course I wouldn't."

Why *of course?* "I don't like rejection," Luke said, and smiled again. "So I just arrived."

"I bet you haven't been rejected in years."

With an edge that surprised him, he replied, "Not since I earned my first million."

"Poor little rich guy."

"That's me. What were you going to have for supper?"

"Scrambled eggs."

"I can offer borscht, capons stuffed with wild rice, and blackberry mousse. Along with a reasonable Merlot."

Her mouth was watering. For the food, she thought hastily. Not for the man who was leaning so casually on her newel post, his dark blue sweater deepening the blue of his eyes. Eyes that were laughing at her, full of the charm she'd professed to despise.

Much too easily for her peace of mind, Kelsey capitulated. "I can't very well tell you to come in, because you already did. The dining room's through there. I'll get a couple of placemats from the kitchen."

He walked down the narrow hall into a small room containing a scarred oak table, four chairs and an old-fashioned sideboard; beyond it was a living room in a barely controlled state of chaos. Cardboard packing boxes, piles of books, clothing and sportsgear... Men's clothes, he thought. Hockey and soccer gear. What was going on?

Looked like she'd just booted her husband out, and his stuff was following him out the door at the first opportunity.

He studied the scuff marks on a pair of skates, his brain in high gear, his curiosity intense. Kelsey wasn't wearing a wedding ring; he always paid attention to that particular detail. Married women had never been on the cards for him. Too complicated. Particularly when there were so many single ones all too ready to play.

Then Kelsey marched into the dining room and put two placemats and a dish of butter on the table. "Cutlery's in the drawer," she said. "I'll get the wine glasses."

He put the bag of food down on the table. Knives, forks and spoons were jumbled together in the drawer. All sterling silver, he noticed, and all badly in need of polishing. As she came back in with the glasses and a corkscrew, he said lightly, "Do you spend so much time organizing other people's stuff that you don't get around to your own?"

"I've had other things on my mind. I'll get some serving spoons."

As she moved past him, the overhead light caught her hair, streaking it copper and bronze. Her hips moved delectably in the tight denim. He heard himself say, with a bluntness that dismayed him, "Why the brown tweed suit? Which should, in my opinion, be tossed in the nearest garbage can."

"Open the bag, Luke. Let's eat."

As she sat down across from him, he said blandly, "I see your train of thought—from one bag to another."

A smile twitched her lips. Those eminently kissable lips. "The suit belonged to my mother," she said rapidly, watching as he put a bowl in front of her and removed the plastic lid. "She was a very pretty woman with the clothes sense of a rhinoceros. Mmm…the soup smells luscious."

"Have some sour cream on it. Do you always wear that suit to work?"

"Only for unattached men with a reputation."

"So there's been gossip in the village about me as well as my mother?"

She took a sip of borscht and closed her eyes in ecstasy. "Not unfounded, in your case."

"I like women. So what?"

"In the plural."

"One at a time," he said, rather more sharply than he'd intended.

"Serial fidelity?"

"Is there anything wrong with that?"

As she shrugged, shadows lingered in the little hollows under her collarbones. He wanted to press his lips into those hollows, find out if her skin was as silky smooth as it looked, smell her hair, trace the slim line of her throat to that other hollow at its base.

Dammit, Luke thought, he needed to bed someone like Clarisse or Lindsay. Hot, slick sex, with no entangling emotions. Too bad he'd cooled both those particular relationships in the last year. Out of—he had to be honest—boredom.

He could always find someone else.

"Serial fidelity must be very convenient," Kelsey said. "For you."

Luke dragged himself back to reality. "The women I date always know the score, because I spell it out for them. If they don't like the rules, they don't have to play the game."

"How sophisticated," Kelsey said in a brittle voice. "Why don't we change the subject? I'd hate for a discussion of your sexual standards—such as they are—to ruin this delicious soup."

There were pink patches high on her cheekbones; her skin swept in creamy curves to the corners of her mouth. But he wasn't going to think about her mouth. "So what are you wearing to work tomorrow, Kelsey? Now that I've found you out."

Her thick dark lashes hiding her eyes, she said calmly, "Jeans, I guess. What were you doing in Hong Kong last week?"

Agreeably, he began to talk about his latest real estate deals along the Pacific Rim. He didn't elaborate on the side trip to Cambodia.

As Kelsey got up to remove the soup dishes and bring some plates from the kitchen, Luke pushed back his chair and wandered over to examine the painting on the far wall. A quite astonishing painting, he realized, his interest quickening as he tried to read the signature. It was an abstract, seething with subdued energy, color escaping from an overwhelmingly dark background in small explosions of delight.

Hearing her come back in the room, he said, "Who painted this?"

"I did," she said reluctantly.

"*You* did?"

She raised her brows. "The dinner's getting cold."

"Recently?" he rapped.

"Six months ago."

More and more he was inclined to believe in an ousted husband. "Do you have more?"

She had a roomful of them upstairs. "A few. Oh, look, asparagus. I adore it. And the wild rice looks scrumptious."

Clarisse had the appetite of a sparrow, while Lindsay was allergic to just about everything. It was fun, Luke thought in faint surprise, to share a meal with someone who appreciated it. Smoothly, he began describing his latest visit to the Guggenheim.

As Kelsey swallowed the last mouthful of mousse, she sat back and said spontaneously, "That was a wonderful meal— the bistro only opened last summer, and I've never eaten there. Thank you, Luke."

She was looking right at him, her eyes the glossy brown of melted chocolate. The warmth in them hitched at his breath.

"You're welcome," he said. She wasn't his type. She was from the backwoods, all excited about a takeout meal. Get real, Luke. He added casually, "Can I see more of the paintings?"

She said grudgingly, "There are three others in the living room. I'll put on some coffee."

Picking his way past a mesh bag of soccer balls and a heap of well-worn cleats, he checked out the other paintings, and felt again the stirring of excitement that genuine creativity called up in him. Each of the three gave that same sense of something desperately striving to burst its bonds. Untutored paintings, yes, but full of raw talent.

Forgetting to watch where he was going, he knocked over a pile of textbooks. A signature leaped out at him, written in an untidy masculine scrawl: Dwayne North.

Kelsey's husband. The reason she painted pictures frantic for release.

Not stopping to think, Luke marched into the kitchen. "What's with the husband?"

"Husband?" she said blankly. "Whose husband?"

"Yours. The owner of the soccer gear."

She gave an incredulous laugh. "I do not have, nor have I ever had, a husband. Ditto for fiancé or live-in lover." And there, she thought, is the story of my life.

His eyes narrowed. "How old are you?"

"Twenty-eight."

"Then the guy who owns the cleats and the chemistry texts can't be your son."

"Gee, you're good at math—must be handy for keeping track of all your women."

Luke wasn't used to being laughed at. He said abruptly, "You should be doing something with your art—what are you waiting for? I can't believe you spend your time cleaning out closets for rich people when you're so obviously loaded with talent."

Her chin snapped up at his tone. "I don't see why my paintings are remotely your business."

"When I see work like yours hung where only you can see it, I get a little irked."

"If this is *irked,* I'd hate to see angry. Coffee's made. You can drink it now or take it with you."

"What's the story, Kelsey? Who owns the cleats and the chemistry books?"

Luke had just treated her to one of the best meals in her life, and she had no reason not to tell him. Other than pure cussedness. "My eldest brother, Dwayne. First year med school. Age twenty-one."

"What's wrong with me? I didn't even think of a brother."

"Like I said, the eldest. Glen's twenty, he's studying computer technology; the hockey gear's his. Kirk's eighteen, he started forestry school a week ago. He took his lacrosse gear with him." She gave Luke a level look. "I brought them up. I'm an expert in teenage psychology and hamburgers with the works. I didn't have the time to flit off to art school every morning once they were on the school bus—I was too busy keeping a roof over our heads."

"They all lived here with you?" Luke said, feeling his way.

"They sure did. I'd just started cleaning out Kirk's room the day you called. Five unmatched socks under the bed, a wedge of mummified pizza and six copies of *Playboy.* I did my best to civilize all three of them, but it was uphill work. And now they're gone." The crazy thing was that she missed them, even though she'd been counting the days until she was free.

"Your parents?"

Her voice flattened. "They both died in a train wreck when I was eighteen. No other relatives. So it fell to me to bring up my brothers." Which was also the story of her life.

"So this was your parents' house?"

"At the time, it seemed best to keep things as normal as possible." With a flick of temper she added, "So now you know why my paintings are hanging on my own four walls."

"You sacrificed ten years of your life for the sake of your brothers?" he said inimically.

"It wasn't a sacrifice! Well, not really. Besides, what choice did I have?"

"Plenty, I'd have thought—you could have left."

"My brothers and I had just lost both our parents," Kelsey said tersely. "I couldn't have lived with myself if I'd abandoned them. And if you don't understand that, I don't know where the heck you're coming from."

Ferociously Luke tried to batten down the emotions roiling in his chest: bafflement, fury and pain. His mother hadn't hung in as Kelsey had. The first eight years of his life had been a study in broken promises.

He said sharply, "How is it the three boys are all off at college and you're still home?"

"Give me time—Kirk just left last week," she retorted. "As you can see, step one is to clean up the house. Then I'll put it on the market."

Luke looked around, taking in the battered table, the faded paint, the general air of a house worn down by use and a lack of money. Hadley was a rundown fishing village; she wouldn't get much for the property. "Then what?"

She glowered at him. "You'll be happy to know I'm planning to go to art school on the proceeds—together with what you're paying me."

"So that's why you changed your mind about working for me?"

"*Pride and Practicality.* Jane Austen, the modern version."

"My offer to double your pay still stands," Luke said.

"I don't take charity."

"Call it support for the arts," he said with a grin.

"You know what bugs me about you? You make me angry enough to spit nickels and then you make me laugh."

You know what scares me about you? he thought. I'm as far from bored as I can be.

He kept this observation to himself. Okay, so Kesley had been dealt a tough hand, and she hadn't folded. Unlike his mother. But she still wasn't his type. Far from it. Too unsophisticated. Too many emotions too close to the surface.

Too real.

So why was he sitting here watching the play of light over her cheekbones, the little dimple at the corner of her mouth when she smiled, the sweet curve of her breasts under her tight shirt? Watching and lusting after her, fire streaking straight to his loins in a way he deplored.

He said at random, "Did you find anything in the boxes you brought home?"

"Oh—I forgot! Yes, I did. An envelope of photographs. What did I do with them?"

His heart lurched in his chest. He didn't have a single photograph of his mother.

Kelsey was rummaging through a pile of papers by the telephone and unearthed a faded brown envelope, which she held out to him. The flap was unglued. She said, following the direction of his eyes, "It was open. I had to look inside to see if it was anything important."

He hated the fact that she'd seen the photos first. As if he couldn't help himself, he pulled one out. A pretty little girl was standing under an apple tree that was in full bloom; she was laughing, clutching a book to her chest. It was, unquestionably, his mother.

Kelsey had busied herself pouring the coffee. But something in the quality of the silence caused her to lift her eyes. Luke was standing like a man stunned, his gaze riveted to the picture in his hands. She felt a surge of compassion so strong it took her aback. Hastily she pushed the cream toward him, watching him shove the photo back in the envelope as though it had bitten him. He said flatly, "I should go."

"What about your coffee?"

"I'll skip the coffee—I'll go back and sort through a couple more boxes."

"Luke," she said with careful restraint, "I wish you'd tell me why this search is so important to you—why you're paying me all this money for dribs and drabs of information about your mother."

His knuckles tightened on the envelope. "You don't need to know why! Just give me anything relating to her and keep your mouth shut in the village."

Hot color stained Kelsey's cheeks. "I don't indulge in local gossip."

He should apologize. He didn't. Instead he dropped the envelope on the table and closed the distance between them in two quick strides. Taking her in his arms, he plundered her mouth, his teeth grazing her lip.

And was lost in the red haze, the furious ache of hunger.

CHAPTER THREE

FOR THE SPACE of two full seconds Kelsey was frozen in Luke's embrace. His arms were tight as steel bands. Through her palms, pressed to his chest, she felt the heat of his body, his muscles' taut strength. She couldn't have escaped if she'd wanted to.

She didn't want to. The hard pounding of his heart beneath her fingertips excited her beyond measure. She'd never been kissed like this in her life, with such searching intensity, such a depth of need and desire. She looped her fingers around his neck, feeling with a shock of pleasure the silken thickness of his hair. When his tongue brushed her lower lip, she opened to him, yearning for him to taste her, to invade her.

His hands moved lower, grasping her hips, thrusting her against another hardness; like flame, desire surged through her veins. Knees weak, she clung to him. Her tongue danced with his, their mouths welded in a kiss that she wanted to last forever.

Then he thrust her away so roughly that she stumbled, bumping her hip against the table. He said harshly, "Forget I did that—it won't happen again. I'll see you at eight-thirty tomorrow."

The image of her shocked face imprinted on his brain, Luke strode down the hall as though all the demons in hell were after him. What had possessed him to kiss her like that? Like a man starved for nourishment. Like an addict needing his fix.

He didn't need her. He didn't need anyone. Never had.

He unlatched the door and stepped outside into the chill star-spangled night. That was what he needed, he thought savagely, a sense of perspective. The stars were good at providing that.

He'd just broken two of his cardinal rules: never get involved with an employee, and never make the first move without explaining the way the game worked. Not that kissing Kelsey North could in any way be called a game. From the moment his lips had found hers he'd been engulfed by her. Absorbed in her. Desperate for her.

Thank God he'd found the strength to walk away from her. And away from her was where he intended to stay.

His car was parked under the trees. He fumbled for his keys in his pocket, then whipped around as he heard steps behind him on the gravel driveway.

Kelsey said jaggedly, "You forgot the photographs."

Her hair was in a wild tumble around her face, her eyes huge dark pools. Through the thin fabric of her shirt he could see the little bumps of her nipples. Goddammit, he wasn't going to kiss her again. He took the envelope from her with the tips of his fingers. "Thanks."

She stepped back, hugging her arms to her chest. "I'm not one of your super-sophisticated Manhattan women, Luke. Don't toy with me like that—kissing me as though I'm the only woman in the world and then dropping me as though I disgust you."

"Disgust?" His laugh had no amusement in it. "If I hadn't dropped you, we'd be making love on the kitchen floor right now."

She took another step back. "Am I supposed to believe that?"

"You know I wanted you."

Shivering, she said in a low voice, "I've never met anyone like you. I don't know what to believe."

He was suddenly pierced with guilt; wasn't she telling him she was way out of her depth? "Go inside—you're cold. I'll see you tomorrow."

With a tiny sound of distress, she whirled and ran for the house. The door slammed shut behind her.

Luke got into his car and drove back to Griffin's Keep, grimly concentrating on the road. He was going to put her right out of his mind. His lifestyle didn't begin to accommodate women like Kelsey North. Never had and never would.

The mansion's dark bulk loomed against the stars, secretive and unwelcoming. Could he blame his mother for running away? Would the contents of the boxes bring him any closer to understanding her?

He went inside, and in the room where he and Kelsey had been working he spread the photos over the table. They were all images of Rosemary as a young girl; she looked happy and carefree. He couldn't ever remember her looking happy like that.

Briefly he buried his head in his hands, his nostrils assaulted with the long-ago smells of the apartment block where they'd lived. Rotting garbage, urine, cigarette butts, the lazy drift of dope.

He'd never have to go back to a place like that. The money he'd made since then guaranteed it. He was safe. As that little boy in a slum apartment block hadn't ever been safe.

THAT NIGHT LUKE went through four more boxes, rewarded by finding some of Rosemary's school reports. *Doesn't like to sit still* and *Stirs up trouble* were repeated themes. It was nearly three in the morning when he trailed upstairs, every limb weighted with exhaustion. But when he fell into bed it wasn't Rosemary who kept him wide-eyed and awake, staring up into the darkness. It was Kelsey.

He loathed how desperate he'd felt, how driven. He liked sex as much as the next man. But he also liked being in control.

Tomorrow—today, rather—he wouldn't lay as much as a finger on her. If she had any sense, she'd wear the brown tweed suit to work.

Trouble was, now he knew what was hidden underneath it. And he could remember all too clearly how she'd opened to his kiss, digging her nails into his nape, her hips pressed to his erection.

Hell, he'd never get to sleep at this rate. With a superhuman effort, Luke forced himself to focus on the trend in oil prices, and eventually he did fall asleep. To dream a long-familiar dream of the shadowy woman who had been his mother. She was holding out a pretty red candy and promising it could be his. As he reached for it, already tasting its sweetness, she snatched it back at the very last minute…

Later, much later, he gradually sank into another dream. One of Kelsey lying naked in a field of summer flowers, opening her arms to him, voluptuous and beautiful.

EVEN THOUGH SHE was tempted to do so, Kelsey didn't wear the brown tweed suit the next morning. But the jeans she chose were loose-fitting, and her sweater enveloped her from throat to hip in bright green wool.

If Luke Griffin made the slightest move toward her, she'd belt him first and then she'd quit.

In January's weak sunlight, Griffin's Keep looked ridiculously like the haunted house of a thousand books and movies. She marched up the front steps and found the door firmly locked.

Yesterday Luke had unlocked it before she'd arrived. Not in the mood for subtlety, she leaned hard on the bell. Once, twice, three times. With absolutely no effect. His car, a sleek Mercedes, was parked by the garage, so she knew he was here.

Had he changed his mind overnight and fired her? If so, would he bother to let her know? He was the great Luke Griffin, accountable to no one.

She banged on the panels of the door, hurting her fist. Her jaw set mutinously, she then walked around the house until she came to the room where they worked. Standing on tiptoes, she peered inside. Empty. So was the kitchen. By now it was a quarter to nine.

Kelsey had slept very badly, her dreams full of enough torrid sex for ten women. The man she'd cavorted with in purple satin sheets that exactly matched her toenails had been Luke, an unabashedly and gloriously naked Luke.

No wonder she felt out of sorts this morning. She stormed back to her car and laid on the horn. Although for all she knew, he slept at the back of the house. She then went through the whole bell-ringing routine again. No Luke, apologetic or otherwise.

Fine. She'd go home and scour Kirk's room from one end to the other.

However, as she thrust the key in the ignition, the sun went behind a cloud and the ugly turrets and pinnacles of Griffin's Keep were shrouded in shadow. It wasn't just a depressing house, she thought, it was downright foreboding.

Maybe Luke had slipped on the stairs and hurt himself? Maybe he was ill? Should she go for help?

Unease nibbling at her composure, Kelsey got out of the car and circled the house one more time. Against the south wall a stout Virginia creeper clung to the worn shingles, climbing all the way to the brick chimney. Partway up, it skirted a window that was open several inches.

She'd been a daredevil climber as a kid, outdoing the boys because she had no fear of heights. She shucked off her jacket, glad she'd worn her hiking boots, and started to climb.

It was a cinch. She placed each foot with care, wrapping her fingers around the stout branches, the exercise warming her, the little adventure lifting her spirits. Her life had been too dull for too long. She should add adventure to the list. Near the top, with a capital A.

The window slid open on its hasp. Kelsey levered herself over the sill, landing with a small thud on the floor.

She was in a bedroom. Luke's bedroom.

He was fast asleep on the double bed, his face buried in the pillows, the sheets twisted around his waist. He was also naked, the light falling over the long curves of his spine.

Her dream had collided with reality. Except the sheets were white, not purple.

Kelsey crept closer across the worn floorboards. His torso was rising and falling with the rhythm of his breathing; his hair lay dark on the pillow. He had, she thought unwillingly, a most impressive set of muscles.

Clearly he wasn't sick. She should go straight downstairs and get to work. Then her heart leaped into her throat as he stirred, muttering something under his breath. She froze to the spot, watching in dismay as he turned over. He rubbed his eyes, their vivid blue focusing on her. As she opened her mouth, with no idea what she was going to say, he said, in a voice still blurred with sleep, "I was dreaming about you—come here."

She gave a startled yelp as he seized her wrist and tugged her toward him. Losing her balance, she fell on top of him, her hands splayed on the sheet, her breasts crushed to his bare chest. He looped one thigh over hers, pinning her down, and buried his hands in her hair, pulling her head down to his. She had time to think, *I'm in bed with a man who's tall, dark and handsome.* Then his lips were locked to hers, moving slick and hot until she dissolved into a pool of longing. She moaned his name in helpless surrender, assaulted by the heat of his body, the shock of bone and muscle and sinew.

With strong fingers he dragged her sweater up to her waist; a shudder rippled along her spine as his palms stroked her back, warm and very sure of themselves. "Your skin," he muttered. "I knew it would feel like silk." Then he was fumbling with the clasp on her bra, freeing her breasts.

As his fingers, those clever fingers, found her nipple, teasing it to the hardness of stone, she closed her eyes, drowning in pleasure and a raging hunger she couldn't possibly have denied. She leaned forward, finding his mouth with hers, greedy to taste, frantic to give.

So she was generous, Luke thought in a rush of gratitude. Hadn't he known she would be? Hadn't he known how perfectly her breast would fit his palm? How the scent of her hair would envelop him?

He had to have her. He'd been a fool last night to think he could walk away from her without a backward look.

Rearing up, carrying her with him, he covered her with his body. His kiss deepened until he could scarcely breathe, his heart hammering in his ears. Or was it her heart? Swiftly he hauled her sweater further up, baring her exquisite breasts, all ivory curves and pink tips in the pale light. As he flicked her nipples with his tongue, desperate to taste her, she arched to meet him, her eyes wide-held, shining dark with desire. Her hips moved beneath him, nearly driving him out of his mind. He thrust once, twice, against the denim of her jeans, and heard the tiny cry as her breath caught in her throat.

He had to have her, Luke thought again, striving to breathe past the tightness in his chest. But not here. Not in this joyless house, in a bed not his own, where he'd been visited by nightmares.

He said jaggedly, "Kelsey, we've got to stop. God knows I want you. But this isn't the time or the place."

Had he ever done anything so against every instinct in his body? So contrary to his own impulses?

Kelsey was clutching him by the shoulders, her nails digging in his flesh. His voice seemed to come from such a long way away that she had to struggle to take the words in. *Stop,* he'd said. *We've got to stop...*

Her body, so lissom, so wanton, was a stranger to her. And it was he who'd brought that about. His skillful mouth, his roaming hands, had changed her into a woman she scarcely knew.

She pushed hard against his chest, shaking her hair back, yanking at her sweater to hide her nakedness. Swiftly Luke brought a hand up to still hers. "Wait," he said huskily, "let me look at you."

"I—"

"You're so lovely… Stroking you is like stroking a pearl, smooth and exquisitely shaped."

Poetry was the last thing she would have expected from Luke Griffin. Dumbstruck, Kelsey watched his eyes wander from her shoulders to her peaked breasts, then lower to the gentle narrowing of her waist and the dip of her navel. The expression on his face brought sudden tears to her eyes. Had anyone ever looked at her like that? As though she was the most beautiful creature in the world?

It was he who then pulled her sweater down. Smiling at her, he patted her on the bottom. "Up," he said. "We're going to finish those boxes today if it's the last thing we do."

How could he switch so quickly from assaulting her with pleasure to everyday practicalities? *This isn't the time or the place…* Did that mean he still wanted to make love to her? His words, those lyrical words that had melted her heart, they must have meant something…mustn't they?

She still had her hiking boots on, she noticed distantly.

"Kelsey, are you okay?"

He was untangling himself from the sheets. He was, as she'd suspected, stark naked. Her eyes skittered away from him. "Fine," she said in a choked voice.

"Coffee," he said authoritatively. "An order from the boss."

Kelsey stood up, her eyes flicking over the unmade bed, the tattered wallpaper. Anywhere but at him, in this dingy, too-small bedroom, where a man's body had drowned her in desire. With a strangled gasp she fled the room, pulling the door shut behind her.

Briefly she leaned against the panels, her cheeks hot with embarrassment. Her exit had been about as undignified as her entrance. Neither had been even remotely sophisticated.

She was beginning to hate that word.

Behind the panels she heard the floorboards creak as Luke moved around the room, and she took to the stairs as fast as she could. He'd better be fully dressed when he came downstairs, or she wouldn't be responsible for the consequences.

She could have eaten him alive, devoured him without a thought for the consequences.

For once, Kelsey was glad to be in the archaic kitchen, where she now had a small area clean enough that making coffee had become a comfortable routine. As the scent of Colombian blend teased her nostrils, she hooked her bra, patted her cheeks with cold water, and tried very hard to think.

Torrid sex. She now knew exactly what it felt like.

Wonderful. Overwhelming. Powerful. Frustrating. Oh, she could go on forever.

But was it what she wanted?

Freedom to be herself, to be on her own, was what she wanted. If torrid sex translated itself into an affair with Luke Griffin—even a short-lived affair—wouldn't she lose something she'd craved for years?

Or would she berate herself for cowardice instead? Sex, so she'd read, was supposed to free the creative impulse, feed the artistic muse. Somehow she didn't think what had happened upstairs in that gloomy bedroom had had much to do with her muse.

With a wry twist of her mouth, Kelsey decided caffeine was necessary for tackling such philosophical issues. But at least she'd distanced herself from that woman in the bedroom who would, in an instant, have begged for more, more, more…

She was seated at the table in the room down the hall, busily working, when Luke wandered in ten minutes later. "Great coffee," he said absently, and sat down at the adjoining table.

Just as if he hadn't kissed her senseless only minutes ago, she thought furiously, flicking through a pile of bank statements and subduing several shrewish replies.

"Did I forget to lock the door last night?" he added. "Is that how you got in?"

"I climbed the Virginia creeper up to your room."

He gave a choked laugh. "A cat burglar—where did you learn to do that?"

"In the ivy on the old oak tree behind our house."

"I must remember to keep the silver locked up when you're around."

"You do that."

"You're cute when you're annoyed."

He was openly laughing at her, teeth gleaming, wrinkles at the corners of his eyes. Her own teeth gritted, she fought against his charm. "I'm glad I amuse you."

"You do more than amuse me—that's the problem," he said. "But why did you bother climbing the creeper? Why didn't you just go home?"

"I thought you might have broken your neck on the back stairs."

"You were worried about me?" he said, taken aback.

She was scowling at him. "Yes."

"Oh," Luke said. He wasn't used to anyone worrying about him; he wasn't at all sure he liked the sensation. "Thanks," he said shortly. "And now we'd better get to work. We'll quit at noon for lunch."

If she was smart, Kelsey thought, she'd quit right now. She took another sheaf of papers out of the box and bent to her task.

She had a delightful profile, Luke decided, her nose straight, her chin with a decided firmness. She was certainly no push-over. Unfortunately, she was no sophisticate either.

He had to have her. That hadn't changed. Even though he'd doused himself in a tepid shower and done his best to conjure up images of Clarisse and Lindsay.

His best hadn't been good enough. They'd dropped off his radar. Kelsey was the one he wanted. And Kelsey wanted him. She was twenty-eight years old, he thought, old enough to know that affairs, by definition, didn't last. Besides, after bringing up three boys, she must be all too ready to break out.

Remembering how she'd clambered up the creeper filled him with amusement at her skill, and sheer terror because she could have fallen.

First things first. Once the weight of these damned boxes was off his shoulders, he'd be able to concentrate.

By noon, he'd found school reports where Rosemary had been getting into far more serious trouble than talking in class, and Kelsey had turned up a newspaper report about Rosemary's second appearance in juvenile court, this time for drinking and driving. Training his face to immobility, he put them to one side. At four-thirty, while Kelsey was in the kitchen brewing another pot of coffee, he came across three letters.

The first was from Rosemary to Sylvia, demanding money and making it clear Rosemary had been banished in disgrace from Griffin's Keep in her third month of pregnancy, with less than a hundred dollars to her name. Sylvia's reply, dated several weeks later, was cold and to the point: she would pay for admission to an addictions clinic, but nothing else. The third letter was Rosemary's furious refusal, laced with invective. From the dates on the letters, he'd been about six.

Addictions clinic. With all his strength Luke fought back images merciless in their clarity. But amidst this turmoil one thing was obvious: at Griffin's Keep the recipe had already been in place. A miserly, heartless mother. A rebellious young girl, full of spirit and hungry for life. An unplanned pregnancy, and exile.

And he, a little boy, caught between two generations.

He buried his face in his hands. How he hated being ambushed by the past like this! He'd overcome the past, or so he'd thought. Wasn't his bank account proof enough?

"Luke! Are you all right?"

Cursing, he raised his head. "Yeah…tired, that's all."

His slumped shoulders, the defeated bend of his neck, had frightened Kelsey. If only he'd share with her what this all meant, she thought painfully. "I brought you a chocolate doughnut," she said, trying to steel her heart against the tension in his jaw and his hooded eyes.

Secrets. She'd never liked them.

She sat down, took a bite of her own doughnut, and went back to work. Four hours later they'd emptied the last box, which yielded three more reports from juvenile court. Luke dumped them on his pile and ran his fingers through his hair. "Thank God that's over."

He looked exhausted, Kelsey thought, yet tense as a coiled spring. She said impulsively, "Luke, let's get out of here. I hate this house."

"You and me both."

"Come to my place. I'll cook supper—although it won't be a gourmet meal like last night. Fish and chips. Glen always says I make the best fish and chips the length of the shore."

Why am I doing this? she thought in horror. After what happened this morning, I'm inviting Luke into my home? Where there are four beds? That's not just crazy, it's suicidal.

Or is it freedom?

How was she supposed to know the difference?

CHAPTER FOUR

TRYING TO WORK the tension out of his shoulders, Luke said, "Dinner at your place? I'll be right behind you, Kelsey, once I've taken a bottle of wine from the cellar. Sylvia Griffin owes me—I might bring two bottles. I tell you, if I never see Griffin's Keep again, it won't be a day too soon."

"I'm with you on that," Kelsey said with a grin, and hurried out to her car.

When Luke arrived, ten minutes after her, she had the curtains drawn against the snow flurries that were whipping past the window, candles were lit on the kitchen shelves, and a semicircle of candles flickered on the dining room table. She had laid the table for two: herself and a man who qualified in spades as tall, dark and handsome.

Which just went to show you shouldn't tempt fate, she thought, or you might get what you asked for. And discover that nothing was quite as simple as you'd expected. She passed Luke the corkscrew. The wine was delicious, full-bodied and fruity; letting it run down her throat, she decided in a rush of rebellion to enjoy herself. Sure, she was out of her depth. But so what? She'd managed to field everything that life had thrown at her so far. Why should Luke be any different?

Swathing herself in an oversize apron that made her feel minimally safer, she began mixing the batter for the fish.

Too restless to sit down, Luke prowled around the kitchen, letting its warmth and friendliness envelop him. There was a calendar from a charity organization on the wall over the phone. He said absently, "That's a very fine orphanage."

Kelsey glanced up. "How do you know? Have you been there?"

"Yeah," he said, wishing he'd kept his mouth shut. "On my last trip to Hong Kong."

"In between real estate deals, you just happened to drop into an orphanage in Cambodia?"

"I told you I was in Cambodia when Sylvia was buried— it's why they couldn't reach me in time."

"Do you support the orphanage?" she asked, frowning at him.

Her big brown eyes precluded easy lies. "I paid to have it built," he said. "The charity runs it."

Her hands stilled. She said shrewdly, "How many other orphanages have you built, Luke?"

"A few. Here and there."

She waved a wooden spoon at him. "How many?"

"Twenty-four. And don't try and make me into some kind of saint."

"There's already a St Luke," she said dryly, "the position's taken. You're not a saint; you're a rich man who cares…and puts the caring into action and cold hard cash."

"Drink your wine," Luke said, then changed the subject. "Can I peel some potatoes?"

She passed him a knife, her eyes velvety warm with approval; she'd donated to that charity for years, her heart wrung by children who by circumstance and violence had been robbed of parents. "The bag's in the end cupboard."

Her apron was shapeless, her sleeves were rolled up and there was a dab of batter on her chin. He wanted to kiss her, Luke thought. Another of those devastating kisses into which he sank and lost himself.

Hastily he located the bag of potatoes in the cupboard and began peeling one. The homely task was oddly relaxing; the ghosts who had been haunting him ever since he'd arrived at Griffin's Keep were gradually receding.

Domesticated, he thought. Undemanding. Not his usual scene.

Kelsey's wrists were slender, blue-veined. If he lowered his head, laid his lips to that little hollow in her ivory skin, he'd be able to feel her pulse, the very voice of her blood.

Even the words he was using were changing, he thought in exasperation. When had he ever felt the urge to spout poetry to any of his female companions?

The short answer was never.

Was he going to take Kelsey to bed tonight, in her own home, surrounded by all the paraphernalia of the three boys she'd raised?

He'd be back in Manhattan tomorrow. Would he then forget about her?

With vicious swipes Luke began slicing the potatoes. Ten minutes later, when they were sizzling in the hot fat, Kelsey said, "Ketchup and tartar sauce in the refrigerator—you could put them on the dining room table. Vinegar, salt and pepper on the counter." Expertly, she flipped a fillet in the pan.

There were two colored photographs held to the refrigerator door by magnets. In one, three husky young men surrounded their sister, all four of them laughing into the camera. In the other, an older couple, also laughing, stood with their arms around each other on the porch of Kelsey's house.

"My parents," Kelsey said. "It's silly, but I still miss them." Her face softened. "They'd been married over twenty years when they died, and loved each other more with each passing day. In a way, it was a good thing they went together…"

Wincing away from all the implications of what she'd just said, unable to think of anything to add to it, Luke took out the sauces and left the kitchen. The living room was still in a state of chaos. Her three paintings drew him like a magnet; gazing at them, he was assailed by a sharp pang of conscience. Take Kelsey to bed and then abandon her without a second thought? He couldn't do it. She wasn't a manipulator, like Clarisse, or all on the surface like Lindsay; Kelsey was pure emotion and sensitivity. Each brushstroke proved it.

He had to have her; every cell in his body impelled him to that end. But at what cost? And on whose terms?

As he turned away, a piece of paper on top of a pile of newspapers caught his eye, partly because the writing was in bright red ink. It was headed THE FREEDOM LIST. Quickly his eyes skimmed the page. *Go to art school. Travel. Paint a masterpiece. Have torrid sex.*

He jolted to a stop. This last directive had been crossed out. *Have an affair* had been printed above it.

His pang of conscience vanished in a surge of relief. So Kelsey wanted an affair; perhaps she had left the list out so he'd read it. If the few kisses they'd exchanged were anything to go by, the sex would indeed be torrid.

Paint a masterpiece. His brain made a lightning-swift leap. His good friend Rico was a world-renowned artist.

"Dinner's ready, Luke," Kelsey called from the kitchen. "Come and get it."

Come and get it... Oh, yes, he thought, and went back into the kitchen.

The fish was tender and flaky, the batter crisp and the French fries, drenched in vinegar and salt, delicious. Luke said soulfully, "Why haven't any of the men in Hadley snapped you up? You're gorgeous and you've got a body to die for— and your fish and chips are the nearest thing to heaven."

"There was the small matter of three boys underfoot, and a dearth of eligible men."

No wonder *torrid sex* had been written in red ink. Luke

said, squeezing lemon juice over his fish, "I noticed your list in the living room—"

"My list?" she squeaked, blanching. "Where? I didn't leave it out, did I? Luke, you didn't read it!"

"You did, and I did." He gave her his most charming smile. "It was difficult not to—the ink's eye-catching. So I have a proposal for you. For both of us, actually. A joint venture."

From ivory-pale, her cheeks had flushed as red as the ink. She said in a rush, "I meant to take it upstairs. But then I must have gotten distracted sorting Glen's old hockey gear. You didn't really read it?"

Do a sales pitch, Luke. Fast. "I own a resort on a little island in the Bahamas," he said with another big smile. "My good friend Rico Albeniz is flying down there later this week to spend a few days—have you heard of him?" When she nodded, he went on, "I'll call him tonight. You and I will fly down there tomorrow, and you can have a lesson or two with him."

"With Rico Albeniz? He wouldn't even *look* at me—he's famous!"

"He'll look at you. If I ask him to."

"Money talks?" she said coldly, forking up some chips.

"He's my friend," Luke said, an edge to his voice.

"Sorry," she muttered. "But—"

"I haven't finished," Luke said patiently. "While we're there, you and I will share a bed. Have an affair. Don't you see? Travel, torrid sex, and the chance to paint—you can cross three things off your list at once."

"How very efficient," she said, in an unreadable voice.

"It's called time-management," he added with a touch of smugness, and took another mouthful of fish.

"Spoken like a businessman."

He leaned forward. "You want me, Kelsey, and I want you—as I swear I've never wanted a woman before. You're as far from my usual kind of lover as you can be, and I should be running in the opposite direction. I don't normally babble on about pearls or orphanages or my mother, and I don't know why I'm doing it with you. But I do know one thing—I won't rest until I have you in my bed."

He seemed to have finished all he had to say. He dabbed his last mouthful of fish in tartar sauce. Kelsey was gaping at him, her fork partway to her mouth, her eyes dazed. "I can't have an affair with—"

"Why can't you?"

"To start with, I can't go away tomorrow. Just like that. I have...responsibilities." Her voice died to a whisper.

"No, you don't. The last one left for forestry school a few days ago."

Kelsey swallowed a French fry that tasted like cardboard. She needed a haircut, she thought crazily, she couldn't go away. "I have to sell the house."

"You'll be in much better shape to do so after a holiday."

"I don't have any—"

"—money? I'm writing you a check this evening for the last three days. The flight's free, because it's on my private jet, and I own the resort—no room charge."

She glared at him. "I wasn't going to say money. I was going to say clothes!"

"Money buys clothes. We'll stop off in Manhattan tomorrow long enough for you to shop."

"The money you're paying me has to go toward art school, not clothes."

"Then *I'll* buy them. You won't need much. A bikini, a sundress or two, a pair of sandals."

"Your money buys *your* clothes," Kelsey announced frostily. "It doesn't buy mine."

"Whose rule is that? And isn't it time you broke it?"

"Oh, stop!" she cried. "We're going around in circles. I'm not going to have an affair with you."

"We made a good start on one this morning."

"I'm not the kind of woman who has affairs."

Not his type. Luke shoved those three little words back where they belonged and said forcefully, "Seems to me you've been looking after everyone but yourself for ten years, Kelsey. Isn't that what your list is all about? I'm offering you a chance to do something new. To break free, rebel, have some fun. To enjoy yourself before you sell the house and hit the books at art school."

He'd pushed every one of her buttons. She bit her lip. "But how would I ever tell my brothers?"

"You won't."

"I've never lied to them in my life."

He raised his brows. "You're not lying to them. You're just not telling them the whole truth. Kelsey, you're not accountable to them—you have a life of your own now. One you've damn well earned."

If only everything he said didn't make such sense. Weakening, but determined not to show it, she said in a hostile voice, "Just how long will this affair last?"

"That depends on both of us, doesn't it?"

"What kind of an answer's that?"

"The only possible answer." Luke held tight to his temper. "There are terms, Kelsey, which are better out in the open from the start. I'm not into marriage or long-term commitment. I'd be faithful to you for as long as we're lovers, and I'd require the same of you. When the time comes to end the affair, I'll be the first to tell you—nothing underhanded, no games."

The words had tripped so easily off his tongue, as if he'd said them many times, she thought, infuriated. Which, of course, he had. "Are you finished?"

His eyes narrowed. "I spend a certain amount of time every day on business matters, and I don't expect to be interrupted."

"Fine. Now it's your turn to listen. Because if I agree to

go—*if,* please note—I'd have terms as well. First, don't ever interrupt me when I'm painting. Second, if I decide to leave the Bahamas before you're ready to have me leave, I want your private jet at my disposal. Third, marriage is the last thing on my mind—freedom's what I'm after, not a wedding ring. Fourth, we'd set a limit on the money spent on clothes, and don't ever think you can buy me." She took a deep breath and gave him a ferocious smile. "I think that's it."

Not his type. Clarisse, Lindsay and the rest had bent over backward to agree to his terms, all the while scheming how they'd change his mind. But Kelsey didn't want commitment at any price. So why was he furious with her when he should be relieved?

"I'll be here at nine-thirty in the morning," he said. "Do you have a passport?"

"I renewed it the day Kirk was accepted at forestry school."

"Good. See you tomorrow. Be packed and ready." Luke turned on his heel and marched out of the room.

She heard the front door squeal on its hinges. She hadn't put enough oil on it, Kelsey thought absently, and knew that subconsciously she'd been expecting Luke to persuade her to go to the Bahamas by using the most basic of means. One kiss was all it would have taken.

Why hadn't he kissed her? And why was she so desperately disappointed?

An affair with Luke Griffin? That wasn't rebellion. It was certifiable madness.

WHEN LUKE ARRIVED the next morning, sharp at nine-thirty, he'd already engaged a real estate agent to put Griffin's Keep on the market, and selected an auction house to clear the place of furniture. He knocked on Kelsey's door and walked in. She was in the kitchen, drinking coffee, her brown eyes wary. She was wearing pencil-slim dark brown pants and a creamy mohair sweater, big copper earrings dangling at her lobes.

He reached up in the cupboard, took out a mug, poured himself some coffee and took a hearty gulp. "I needed that," he said. "Thank God I'll never have to set foot in my grandmother's kitchen again. We'll take a helicopter into town. Are you ready?"

Biting back any number of retorts, Kelsey said coolly, "You're assuming I've decided to go?"

"I'm prepared to throw you over my shoulder if you haven't," he said with a wolfish grin.

"You can spare yourself the trouble—my bag's packed."

"Charm plus sex—you couldn't resist."

She gave him an amiable smile. "Crossing three things off the list. That's what I couldn't resist."

"Maybe we should make a start on one of them," he said, and took two steps toward her. Putting his arms around her, pulling her to his body, he kissed her on the mouth. The taste of her ripped along his nerves; lust clawed its way through his body, hot and sharp. As he teased her lips open, her breath fanned his cheek, warm, enticing. Tangling his fingers in her hair, he drank deeply, his tongue flicking hers, his groin hard as iron.

She was going to be his, in a place of his choice and on his terms. That was all that mattered.

Her hips were pressed to his erection, inflaming him; his heart was beating in thick, heavy strokes. Starved for her, he clasped her by the waist, the softness of her breasts crushed against his ribcage. Her palms had cupped his face; locked, he devoured her, and knew the harsh, panting breaths he could hear were his own.

But he wasn't going to take her here. That wasn't the plan. The blood roaring in his ears, Luke made himself gradually draw back, pushing aside the collar of her sweater to lick the frantic pulse at the base of her throat, then skimming her jaw with his lips. She was trembling, he realized, and slowly lifted his head.

Her eyes were clouded with desire. With his fingertip he traced the moist, swollen curve of her lower lip, trying without success to calm his own heartbeat. He said unsteadily, "Torrid? Oh, yes…"

She blinked. "I didn't know what that word meant until I met you."

"You only know the half of it."

"If there's more, I won't be able to stand up."

"You'll be lying down," he said, sliding his hand over the elegant rise of her cheekbone.

Shivering, she said in a rush, "You frighten me, Luke. What you do to me, how I feel when you kiss me—how will I bottle that up when you decide you've had enough of me?"

"I once spent ten months in a home run by nuns. Sister Elfreda had a saying: don't borrow trouble."

He'd done it again, Luke thought. Told her something he never talked about. He'd loved Sister Elfreda; at least he hadn't spilled that particular secret.

"The week of living dangerously," Kelsey said dryly. Wasn't Sister Elfreda one more clue to the enigma—the increasingly fascinating enigma—that was Luke Griffin?

THREE HOURS LATER Kelsey was standing, stripped to her underwear, in a fitting room so luxurious she could scarcely concentrate on the clothes. Luke was sitting outside, patiently waiting for her. Luke and his platinum credit card.

The frighteningly well-groomed buyer of women's wear unsnapped Kelsey's bra and slipped a sundress over her head. The skirt was flirtatiously brief, the bodice almost non-existent.

A linen halter dress followed it, then a full-length silk skirt and a draped tunic that swished gently as she moved. Sandals, flat and stiletto-heeled, plain and bejeweled; silk underwear edged with lace so fine Kelsey was afraid she'd tear it by looking at it; bikinis, some of which verged on the indecent.

Then she fell in love with a straw sunhat whose brim framed her face deliciously, and a tiny evening purse flashing with fake jewels that was perfect with the silk skirt. Panic-stricken, Kelsey looked at the price tags, hauled on her own clothes and hurried out of the fitting room. Luke was sitting in a velvet chair, his face buried in the financial section of the newspaper. She gasped, "Luke, I'm spending far too much money. We should go somewhere cheaper."

He lowered the paper; in his pinstripe suit he looked at home here in a way she didn't. "Do you like the clothes?"

"Of course! That's not the issue."

"Kelsey, it would take you a year of concentrated shopping to make even a dint in my pocketbook. Buy whatever you like—including something for a January day in Manhattan. Because we'll go somewhere for a late lunch before we fly out. And, please, smother that scrupulous conscience of yours. This is about enjoying yourself."

Enjoying yourself... How could she not, surrounded by such richly hued fabrics and impeccable tailoring? This was also about rebellion, she thought, and marched back into the fitting room. Swiftly she made her selections, then said to the buyer, "And I want a nightgown, which I'll pay for myself."

The one she chose was pale coral, the skirt slit to mid-thigh, the bodice seductively cupping her breasts. Ten minutes later she emerged again, this time wearing a tangerine coat with gold buttons, over knee-high leather boots and a cashmere dress that she adored.

"I'm ready," she said breathlessly.

Luke looked up. Something flashed in his eyes. "Lunch at the Ritz-Carlton in Battery Park," he said. "Fabulous views of the Statue of Liberty, and you'll be the most beautiful woman there."

Her vision wavered with sudden tears. She blinked them back; but ten minutes later, when they were seated in Luke's limousine, she said raggedly, smoothing the soft wool of her coat, "Luke, there's no way I can thank you—for this, and all the other clothes you bought me."

"You don't have to."

"I feel like a princess." Her smile was unsteady. "My coat would match the pumpkin."

"Show me your dress."

She unbuttoned her coat; the taupe dress was staggeringly, expensively simple. "Hmm," he said, then spoke briefly to his chauffeur. They drew up outside a stone façade on Fifth Avenue. "Wait here," Luke added.

He was back in ten minutes, a flat box in his pocket. Once they were seated in the bar on the fourteenth floor, and had dealt with a menu that opened whole new vistas to Kelsey, he put the box in front of her. "To go with the dress," he said.

Her lashes flickered as she saw the name of the jeweler. Inside the box was a gold collar of delicate fretwork, with bracelet and earrings to match, their intricacy a perfect foil for her dress. This time tears hung on her lashes, sparkling like diamonds in the light from the wide windows. "They're gorgeous," she whispered. "Will you put them on for me?"

Luke pushed back his chair. He'd given many gifts to many women over the years. None had ever made the recipient cry nor, he had to be honest, given him so much pleasure in the choosing. His fingers brushing her nape, he fastened the clasp on the collar, then circled her wrist with the bracelet. "The earrings I'll leave up to you," he said.

She fumbled with them, the cool gold bumping against her neck. If she and Luke had been alone now, she would have gone to him without an instant's doubt. Not because he'd spent money on her. It wasn't nearly that crude or that simple. Rather because of the look in his eyes when he'd mentioned Sister Elfreda; because of the slight unsteadiness in his fingers as he'd fastened the bracelet around her wrist.

She only hoped that when the time came she would feel as confident, as certain that what she was doing was right for both of them.

CHAPTER FIVE

NINE HOURS LATER, Kelsey and Luke were finally alone, strolling along a path covered with finely crushed shells which led from the resort to Luke's private villa. The pale trunks of royal palms lined the path. Kelsey's head was whirling like the blades on the helicopter that had whisked them from the small airport near Hadley to Manhattan; it felt like a lifetime ago.

She was wearing her new linen halter dress, her bare shoulders covered with a delicate silk shawl, her throat encircled with the gold collar Luke had given her. She'd just eaten a four-course meal in the lofty, luxuriously appointed dining room. Stars punctured a sky of black velvet. The soft *shoosh* of waves collapsing on the sand fell on her ears, while the exotic scent of frangipani drifted to her nostrils.

She was a long way from Hadley.

She was a nervous wreck.

It was ridiculous. Once Luke kissed her she wouldn't have a thing to worry about: he'd sweep her off her feet. She was counting on it. Certainly he had more than enough experience for both of them.

Was that the problem—that already she was comparing herself to the icy blonds and sleek brunettes who were his usual companions? She might be dressed as elegantly as any of them, but underneath she was still Kelsey North from Hadley.

Afterward, when the sex was over, how would she extricate herself gracefully? She groaned inwardly. Pretend to fall asleep? Run for the bathroom and lock the door? Do it again?

And what signals was she supposed to be sending out right now? Shouldn't she be flirting with him, leaning into his body, sending him suggestive glances? Hurry up and kiss me, Luke, she silently pleaded. We both know I can't think when you do that, and right now I'm thinking too much. Much too much.

"It's a lovely night, isn't it?" she said, in a voice that sounded completely artificial.

They turned a corner in the path, and there was the villa in front of them, with its pastel pink walls and white columns, its hibiscus, bougainvillea and heart-shaped orchids. Her own heart was doing its best to force its way out of her chest; if Luke couldn't hear it, he must be deaf.

Stop it, she scolded herself. *You've come all this way to make love with Luke. It's a risk worth taking.*

Luke opened the tall front door and ushered Kelsey into a foyer that had a cathedral ceiling and a cool ceramic floor. He'd always loved this house, even though it didn't quite measure up to his Tuscan villa.

As he flicked the switch, a soft gold light fell on Kelsey's face. She didn't look like she was enjoying his tropical paradise, he thought with another of the disconcerting stabs of doubt that had been attacking him for the last couple of hours. She'd kept up a stream of chatter throughout dinner, picking at her food, and now she was vibrating with nerves. She looked, to put it bluntly, terrified.

Terrified of him.

The thought curdled his gut. Perhaps he'd taken her completely out of her depth by bringing her here, emphasizing—cruelly—the gap between her circumstances and his. Would it have been better had he started their affair in her little house in Hadley, despite village gossip? Surely she wouldn't have looked so terrified back home in her own bedroom?

It was too late for that now. Making an instant decision as he opened the door to the east wing, he said calmly, "You look tired, Kelsey—it's been a long day, hasn't it? I think we should postpone the torrid sex for now. I'll order breakfast to be delivered here at nine in the morning, then you're booked into the spa at ten, for the whole day. We can meet for dinner before Rico arrives. Sleep well, won't you? Enjoy yourself tomorrow."

He kissed her chastely on the cheek, turned on his heel and closed the door behind him.

He'd done the right thing. The sensible and considerate thing. Or was he being a fool to turn his back, even temporarily, on a woman whose body haunted him day and night?

He was putting her needs ahead of his, he realized, his footsteps slowing as he walked down the vaulted corridor to his own room. Which was, for him, a first.

But he wasn't being entirely altruistic. When he took Kelsey to his bed he wanted it to be perfect, for both of them. By the looks of it, he was willing to wait for that to happen.

Fool or not.

TOO CONFUSED TO be angry, too tired to cry, Kelsey walked down the hall to her bedroom, closed yet another door and went to bed. Through the louvered windows the sea whispered to the sand and the palm fronds gossiped together. A bird squawked in the bushes, then fell silent.

Luke had kissed her on the cheek as though he was her brother, not her potential lover. She should know. She had three brothers.

She didn't want to be treated like Luke's sister.

Defiantly she lay down in the exact center of the vast bed. She felt far from home and very much alone; it took her a long while to get to sleep.

But when she woke sunlight was lancing through the wooden louvers and Kelsey's spirits rose. Maybe S for sex wasn't happening, but H for holiday sure was, she thought, and lifted the cover from her silver breakfast tray. Papaya, mango and fresh pineapple juice, along with fluffy scrambled eggs and homemade pastries. None of which she'd prepared herself.

She bit into a crisp, flaky chocolate croissant. She'd swim in the villa's pool to work it off, after her day at the spa.

A whole day at a spa. She gave herself a little hug of anticipation.

She and Luke would work things out. Of course they would.

SEVEN HOURS AFTER breakfast, Kelsey was back in her room. The spa sessions had ended with a facial, shampoo and haircut, including a massage of her scalp that had blissed her out. The whole day had been blissful, she thought, gazing at herself in the mirror. She looked—and felt—like a new woman.

On impulse, she pulled open the drawer of her dresser and took out the nightgown she'd bought in Manhattan. Slipping out of her clothes, she pulled it over her head, and again looked at herself in the mirror.

A stranger, a beautiful, glowing stranger, looked back at her. But it wasn't a stranger. It was herself.

Then, with a clutch at her nerves, she heard someone tap on her door, and heard the voice that had haunted her dreams. "Kelsey? It's Luke."

She could have said *Wait a moment*. But wasn't it inevitable he was here? She opened the door and smiled at him, and at the look on his face she melted.

"I was going to ask if you wanted to go for a swim," he said thickly, his gaze raking her from head to toe.

Her hair framed her face in soft chestnut curls; her eyes looked huge and exotic, her cheeks delicately flushed beneath thick, dark lashes. She was smiling, her mouth a luscious curve. Then there were all those other curves, Luke thought, his mouth dry. Silk clinging to the rise of her breasts, shadowing the valley between them; silk skimming her hips and the long line of her thighs. Her feet were bare, her toenails painted a soft coral pink.

She said, her voice with a little catch in it, "I don't think I want to go for a swim right now."

"What would you like to do, Kelsey?"

She did what she'd longed to do last night: stepped closer to him, ran her fingers up his chest and laced them around his neck. "I'm expecting you to show me."

The terror was gone, he thought, although not the shyness. "There's nothing in the world I'd rather do," he said huskily, and stepped inside, latching the door behind him. Then he bent his head to kiss her.

She met him more than halfway, her lips parting, her tongue seeking his in a sudden explosion of heat that had him reeling. He wrapped his arms around her, drawing her the length of his body, all warmth and delicious silk, all eagerness and trembling. Had he ever wanted a woman as he wanted this one?

Never.

Lissom and willing, she pressed into him, the soft weight of her breasts inflaming him, shredding his vestige of control. Lifting her, he carried her over to the bed, where he ripped back the covers and laid her on the smooth sheets. Her hair smoldered on the pillows like a banked fire as she held out her arms to him. For a moment he stood there, undoing the buttons on his shirt, drinking in her beauty. Then he tossed the shirt on the floor, following it with his cotton trousers and briefs. Naked, fully aroused, he lowered himself and covered her. And shuddered from pent-up hunger.

This time when he kissed her their tongues danced, their breath mingling. She smelled sweetly of flowers, the cool silk and her warm skin igniting him like wildfire. He pushed at the thin straps of her gown, baring her shoulders to his touch, burying his lips in the hollow below her collarbone, on the pulse at her throat, where her blood sang of need and a hunger that matched his. Then he pushed the rippling silk to her waist, baring her breasts. With exquisite gentleness, watching her face, he stroked the ivory slopes to their tips.

She whimpered his name, arching to meet his caress. Flicking her nipple with his tongue, he heard with a primitive thrill her sharp indrawn breath. Taking her in his mouth, drawing deep on her sweetness, he felt her judder beneath him. "Luke," she gasped. "Oh, God, Luke…"

He raised his head long enough to push her gown down her hips. With one quick motion she freed herself from its folds. On the apple-green sheets her thighs gleamed white, joining in a dark triangle that he ached to explore. Suckling her other breast, its nipple hard as a shell from the beach, he let one hand wander to her navel, then lower, seeking her, sensing her open her legs to him and welcome him. She was all wetness and heat; he drew back, fighting the temptation to plunge into her and make her his own in the most elemental of ways. There was time. All day and all night to possess the woman whose writhing hips were driving him crazy.

She was his. He knew that already.

Her hands were roaming his torso, tangled in his chest hair, lingering on muscle and bone, as though she, too, was on a voyage of discovery. They slipped lower, to the jut of his hip, then lower still, until she was encircling him. Another shudder shook Luke's body; for a moment, head bowed, he was still, overwhelmed by pure sensation.

"Should I stop? Do you want—"

"Want?" he said hoarsely. "You don't need to even ask, Kelsey. Do whatever pleases you…"

With that trace of endearing shyness, she took his hand

in hers and guided it between her legs. As he touched her, searching out her center, then stroking its slickness, her eyes widened to wells of darkness. Her breathing caught in her throat. She sobbed his name once, then twice, teetering on the very edge of a whirlpool of dark, desperate needs.

He bent to kiss her, laving her with his tongue, and all the while his fingers rhythmically, almost hypnotically, were spinning her out of control. She cried out, then screamed, her body bucking beneath him, and peaked with a shattering intensity.

Luke's heart was thudding in his chest. Her face, drowned, open and vulnerable, was so beautiful that his throat clogged with emotion. He watched as slowly, gradually, she came back to him. She said unsteadily, "I wasn't expecting... I didn't—"

"You were perfect. And, Kelsey, there's more."

Whoever her previous lovers had been, he thought, they hadn't cared for her enough that she felt entitled to pleasure; he felt a hot stab of anger toward those unknown men. So wasn't it up to him to repair the damage? Not giving her time to think, he drew her down to lie beside him, cupping her buttocks and pressing her into his erection, then kissing her lips, her cheekbones, her throat, nipping her flesh and scraping it gently with his teeth, imprinting her.

"I still want you," she whispered, rubbing her breasts against him, throwing one leg over his and clamping him to her with a possessiveness that nearly wrecked him. Holding fast to a remnant of control, he slid lower down her body, sampling the silken skin, the rise of hip and juncture of thigh, with its mossy dampness and warmth. This time she rose and fell in a single sharp cry of completion, her nails digging into his hips, her head thrown back. Only then did he drive into her.

And meet resistance.

As pain flashed across her face, his heart lurched in his

chest; incredulity ripped through him. *No,* he thought. No. "Kelsey—you're not a virgin?"

For a moment her lashes flickered to hide her eyes. Then she looked up, meeting his gaze. "Yes. I am. But—"

"You've never made love before?" he repeated, stunned.

She flushed. "That's what being a virgin means, Luke. But it doesn't—"

"Why didn't you tell me?" he rapped, rolling off her and rearing up on one elbow.

She half sat up. "I didn't know how."

"It doesn't seem very complicated to me," he said through gritted teeth.

"*Oh, by the way, Luke, I've never been with a man before*— it's not exactly something you discuss at the dinner table."

"That's why you were so strung out last night," he said. "I just thought you were overtired."

"I was scared out of my wits."

"Where have you been all your life? You're twenty-eight, for God's sake."

Her heart clenched like a cold fist in her ribcage. Taking refuge in temper, she said, "You saw the set-up. After my parents died, I raised three young boys in a very small village. How was I supposed to meet anyone? The few dates I had took one look at Dwayne, Glen and Kirk and instantly lost my phone number. Oh, I could have wrestled with some guy in the back seat of a car—that's always available, no matter how small the village— but I was brought up to believe sex was important, not something you did casually, like changing your socks. So no lovers, Luke. Until you came along and offered me torrid sex in the tropics."

"The offer no longer stands," he said curtly. "I don't do virgins."

Kelsey sat up straight, forgetting her nudity in a flood of sheer rage. "For the first time since we met, I feel cheap. Thanks a lot."

"Dammit, I kept my distance until I saw your list—because you weren't my type. Not sophisticated enough, too emotional. But after I'd read how you wanted an affair I figured that was enough of a go-ahead."

"You're acting as though being a virgin is something I should be ashamed of!"

He raked his fingers through his hair. "It's not," he said shortly. "But virgins definitely aren't my type. Hell, Kelsey, I'd feel like a louse if I—"

"Even if I wanted you to?" she interrupted, her chin tilted, her cheeks bright scarlet.

"That's got nothing to do with it."

"Seems to me it has *everything* to do with it." Abandoning pride, speaking from the heart, Kelsey said passionately, "Luke, I want you…I had no idea I could want anyone the way I want you. Please, make love to me." Her eyes softened, deepened. "Someone has to be first, and I'd be proud and very happy if it was you."

Although his whole body was one big ache of frustration, Luke said in a raw voice, "No—I can't do that."

She flinched. "Why not?"

"Your husband, fiancé, boyfriend—the man you're going to spend the rest of your life with—he's the one you should lose your virginity with. Because you're the marrying kind, Kelsey. I know you are."

"What if I don't want to wait for this mythical husband? What then?"

"I'm not into marriage. I've been clear about that from the start."

"But you're the man I happen to be naked in bed with right now," she said tightly.

"That's easily fixed," he said, and got up and reached for his trousers. After pulling them up, he snapped them at his waist.

"So that's it?" Kelsey said in a thin voice.

"Don't you see? I'm trying to do the right thing here!"

"According to you," she said bitterly, crossing her arms over her breasts.

"I'm the one who gets to live with my conscience." God, he sounded pompous, Luke thought savagely, picking up his shirt from the floor. "Rico's coming in late tonight, so we'll all meet at breakfast tomorrow," he said. "Why don't you join me for dinner later this evening—around eight?"

In public, she thought. Fully clothed, with no chance of seduction. "Fine," she said, praying he'd leave, because in two minutes she was going to indulge in a crying jag. A big one. Or else throw that very expensive vase of flowers at the wall in the hopes the glass would smash into a million pieces.

Had she ever felt so humiliated in her life? So frustrated?

Had she ever been so resoundingly rejected?

No, to all three. Particularly the last. Right now she didn't care if she never saw Luke Griffin again.

CHAPTER SIX

LUKE STRODE DOWN THE HALL as though a hundred angry women were on his case. He'd done the right thing, the only thing. He had to believe that, even if Kelsey didn't.

After crossing the courtyard, he stopped by the side of the long, rectangular pool that occupied the U of the villa, and dipped his fingers in. The water was gently, tropically warm. If it had been cooler he would have jumped in: the villa's equivalent of a cold shower. Ice-cold would be best. Frigid.

Virginal Kelsey might be. Frigid, she wasn't.

At breakfast tomorrow he'd introduce Rico to Kelsey. Then he'd claim the press of business and hightail it north, back to Manhattan and women like Clarisse.

As for Kelsey, she could cross painting and travel off her list. Two out of three ain't bad, he thought. Some other man would have to give her the torrid sex.

Some other man... The bastard had better be good to her. Luke's fists clenched at his sides, and his chest felt tight. Some other man smoothing the sweet rise of her breast, watching the storm gather in her face, then hearing her cry out with release...

How could he be jealous of a man he'd never met? Worse, how could he feel the hollow ache of missing her when he hadn't even left yet?

He straightened in sudden decision. He'd go and tell her now that he was leaving, get it over with. Better now than in front of Rico in the morning. Then maybe, just maybe, he'd be able to sleep.

When he reached Kelsey's bedroom door, Luke hesitated outside. What if she were already asleep? The last thing he wanted to do was wake her. Very carefully, he put his ear to the door.

His whole body tensed. She was weeping. The harsh, ugly sobs of true pain. Oh, God, he thought, now what do I do?

Very quietly, he opened the door. Kelsey was on the bed, her arms wrapped around her knees, her forehead resting on them. She was sobbing as though her heart would break.

Following his instincts, Luke crossed the room in four quick strides, knelt on the bed and took her in his arms. As she froze in shock, another sob catching in her throat, he murmured, "Kelsey, it's okay…don't cry, please don't cry."

"I feel so s-stupid," she wailed. "I should have told you about being a virgin when you first saw the list, but I thought you'd laugh at me. You're so experienced, all those different women, while all I know about is hockey practise and dirty socks. I'm sorry, Luke, I've ruined everything. I'll go home tomorrow. I should never have come."

"It's not you who should be apologizing," he said forcefully. "I stormed out of here like a kid who didn't get his own way. But I was stunned when I realized you'd never made love before—you're so beautiful, so desirable. That I should be the first one—it blew me away. So I reacted like a typical male."

Another ragged sob shivered through her. "I wanted you to be the first one."

"I will be—if you still want that," Luke said, his words echoing in his ears. What was going on? Why had he changed his mind so drastically?

Her body stilled. Then she raised her head, scrubbing at her eyes. "Do you really mean it?"

"Yeah, I mean it."

"Oh." She produced a watery smile. "I must look a wreck…you're sure?"

"It's dark," Luke said comfortingly; the brief tropical twilight had faded while he'd stood by the pool. "Wait here."

In the bathroom he wet a facecloth with warm water, then went back into the bedroom. Kelsey was sitting on the edge of the bed, blowing her nose. It was the least romantic of actions; he felt compassion slice through him, mingled with another emotion he wasn't sure he could or wanted to label.

Turning her toward him, he smoothed the cloth over her face, her closed lids, her forehead, his other hand gently kneading her shoulder. "I'm sorry I made you cry."

"I'm sorry I didn't tell you."

"Then we're quits," he said. "I'll be as gentle with you as I know how, Kelsey."

She wrinkled her nose. "Not too gentle," she said, and leaned forward and pressed her mouth to his.

Inexperience coupled with courage: touched to the heart, Luke moved his mouth over hers, smoothing, nipping, savoring. He wanted to give her the very best he was capable of, he thought with a small shock of surprise; she more than deserved that of him.

Her tongue delicately traced his lower lip, sending a lance of heat through his veins. Her nails dug into his nape, her breasts brushing his chest with lingering sensuality. He muttered against her mouth, "Keep that up and you'll be in trouble."

"Promises, promises," she whispered.

Promises… He blanked any thought of his mother's string of broken promises from his mind. This was about Kelsey, who, he'd stake his life on it, was a keeper of promises. "Actions speak louder than words. Is that what you're saying?" he asked, and deliberately cupped her silk-clad breasts in his palms, taking her nipples between his fingers and caressing them until she was moaning deep in her throat.

She'd bewitched him, he thought, with her beestung lips and chestnut curls. He said huskily, "Take off your gown, Kelsey. Show me your body."

She eased away from him. "You first," she said, and began unbuttoning his shirt, her fingertips feathering his chest. Pushing the shirt from his shoulders, she began kissing him, following the arch of bone and ripple of muscle, suckling and teasing. Then she laid her palm flat to his ribcage. "I can feel your heartbeat," she murmured. "I— It makes me feel so powerful, knowing I can arouse you like this…just by being myself."

"No *just* about it." He took her hand, guided it lower. "Aroused, did you say?"

She closed her eyes, clasping all his need for her, moving her hand with exquisite gentleness along the shaft. "Can I die from pleasure?"

"I'm going to beat you to it," he groaned. "God, Kelsey, what are you doing to me?"

Suddenly she laughed, a cascade of delightful sound. "Make love to me, Luke, show me everything I've been missing."

"I always did like a challenge."

He lay back on the bed, drawing her to lie on top of him, his hands spanning her waist. "Only one rule—that you feel free to do whatever you want."

"How will I know if you like it?"

"You'll know."

Hovering over him, her hair tickling his skin, Kelsey kissed him, learning the contours of his face, the strong column of his throat. Made bold by the darkness, she moved lower, overwhelmed with sensation. The hard planes and angles of his body, so inescapably male, entranced her; the depth of ribcage and concavity of his lean belly were her complement. Her breast to his hipbone, her hip to his thigh…how could she have enough of him? Gently she encircled him again, feeling her whole body judder to his silken hardness.

He gasped her name, gripping her by the shoulders. "You'd better stop. Or—"

"Touch me, Luke. Here. And here."

He pulled her higher, opening her thighs to plunder her waiting heat, her whimpers echoing in his ears. And then his restraint broke. Whipping her onto her back, he found that heat again, this time with his tongue. Like flame, Kelsey was born aloft, flaring, flying, until she could bear it no longer. With a strangled cry she buried her fingers in his hair and fell.

Then he was on top of her, hovering over her with his big body. "I want to bury myself in you—I swear I've never desired anyone as I desire you."

Beneath him, she moved her hips to take him in. Her blood was thrumming in her ears; her heartbeat threatened to deafen her. Take me, take me, she thought. Make me yours.

In another surge of fire, she felt Luke edge her thighs apart and ease himself between the slick petals of her flesh. Felt that first imperative thrust.

So this is what it's like to have a man enter you, she thought in wonderment, and opened herself, body and soul, to him. The briefest resistance, a stab of pain, then she was filled with him.

"Kelsey, are you—"

"Yes, oh, yes. Oh, Luke, Luke…"

Her untutored movements, frantic for completion, were driving him to the brink. He touched her once, twice, her slender frame taut as a bow, her muscles clamped around him until he could no longer bear it. Thrust followed thrust, slamming through him. Then came the tumult of release as he emptied within her.

Her cries mingled with his. But the last hoarse cry he heard was his own.

Luke lowered himself to her, burying his face in her hair, his breath rasping in his throat.

Kelsey lay very still. His weight, the hammerbeat of his heart, the sweat sleek on his chest…would she ever forget this moment? This man? Impossible, she thought, and felt a distant flicker of fear.

She pushed it away. "Is it always like that—so powerful? So overwhelming?"

"We'll have to do it again and see—just give me a minute."

"Again?"

He lifted himself on his elbows, gazing down at her flushed cheeks and dazed eyes; amusement lurked in his own eyes. "Unless you don't want to?"

It was, she thought, an odd moment to be suddenly swamped with shyness. "You're so beautiful," she whispered, running her fingertip along the taut slope of his shoulder. "I had no idea…"

"I take it that's a yes?"

"You bet," she said, with such artless enthusiasm that he began to laugh.

"Next time we'll go slower," he said, "take our time. It's called seduction."

"You just have to look at me to do that," she said in a low voice.

He eased free of her, rolling to the other side of the bed. "Candles," he said. "I saw a couple on your dresser. I want to see you, Kelsey."

Minutes later, the small blue flames were flickering their shadows on the ceiling, and over the body of the woman still lying on the bed. The woman he had mated with, Luke thought, male to female, hunger matching hunger.

And would mate with again. Leaning over the bed, he lifted her in his arms and carried her over to the full-length mirror on the wall. Letting her slide to the floor, he drew her in front of him, holding her around the waist, smoothing his hands over her hips and breasts with slow, hypnotic strokes. Trembling in his arms, desire uncurling in her belly, Kelsey leaned into him and surrendered.

Then Luke turned her to face him and began kissing her, his hands still roaming her body. Seared by the liquid blue fire of his eyes, Kelsey met kiss with kiss, caress with caress. She knew better what to expect now, freeing an innate generosity and abandon that filled her with wild joy. Luke, sensing the change, in turn unleashed a passion he'd scarcely known he possessed, bringing her to a stunning orgasm in moments.

Her drowned face, her slender frame so fluid to his touch, were staggeringly beautiful to him. Because her own demands were no less than his, her passion inciting him, he was flooded by a hunger lethal in its intensity; he lifted her, her thighs clasping his, and took her fiercely, swiftly, with bruising strength.

His heart racketing in his chest, his body feeling boneless, drained, Luke said jaggedly, "So much for slow—we didn't even make it to the bed. I didn't hurt you, did I, Kelsey?"

With a breathless laugh she said, "I'm not sure I'll ever be able to move again. But other than that, no, you didn't hurt me. I love everything you do."

"Next time we'll go slow..."

Her cheeks pink, Kelsey faltered, "I didn't think—I mean, I thought after we'd done it once we'd—and now it's twice..."

"Twice, hmm?" Suggestively, he licked her earlobe, then slid his mouth to hers, kissing her with lingering pleasure. "How about I order dinner and we eat in bed? Then we'll see what happens after that."

She gave another of those delighted laughs. "Luke, I'm having a lovely time with you."

She looked, he thought, like a woman who had been well and truly made love to. She looked happy.

He'd done that. If humility was new to him, so too was the edge of unease, of responsibility. Smothering all three, he picked up the phone to order room service.

TEN HOURS LATER Luke woke to the racket of a cuckoo outside the window. He was curled, spoon-fashion, around Kelsey, one thigh over hers, his arm heavy over her ribs, his palm warm on her breast. She was deeply asleep.

He never slept with his mistresses. Too intimate, he'd decided long ago, too easy to misinterpret. Better to keep a safe distance from the start.

So why, after a third, languorous lovemaking, during which—he remembered with aching clarity—he'd dribbled champagne over Kelsey's breasts and belly and then licked it off, had he fallen asleep in her arms?

He was all too ready to make love to her right now. For the fourth time. When would he have enough of her?

He shifted uneasily. He had work to do this morning, and she'd be spending the day with Rico. Just as well, he thought. Time out. Breathing space. To collect his wits and establish a few boundaries.

He was in danger of getting involved with her at a level new to him, an unwanted level. You'd better watch it, he told himself, wishing the cuckoo would shut up.

Carefully he began easing his body away from Kelsey's. She whimpered in her sleep, then suddenly jerked awake, clutching his hand, twisting her head around to stare at him. "Luke!" she said foolishly. "I didn't know where I was, or— I've never woken up in bed with a man before. It's morning already. How did that happen?" With an embarrassed grin she answered her own question. "Because I was exhausted, that's how."

He found himself grinning back. "Can't imagine why."

She blushed endearingly, moving her hips against his groin. "You're not exhausted—I can tell."

"I've got to make some phone calls, then we have to have breakfast and meet Rico, and then I have a meeting scheduled with the resort staff," he said. Making nonsense of his own words, he turned her around to face him and slid inside her.

A frisson rippled the length of her spine; her eyes darkened as a fierce ache of longing swamped her. Deeper and deeper she took him in, until she was filled with him. Panting, closing hard around him, she lost herself in blue eyes the color of the sky.

Luke's face contorted as his own inner throbbing captured him, relentless, uncontrollable. Her whimpers, her heat, her welcome: he was surrounded by her, he thought dazedly, and surrendered, feeling her fall with him.

His breathing harsh in his ears, Luke closed his eyes. So much for time out. So much for distance. She'd bewitched him, with her eyes like woodland pools, her hair like banked fire. Her body like that of a goddess.

She was a woman, he thought fiercely. Just a woman.

"Luke…is something wrong?"

He forced himself to meet her gaze. "Not a thing. Who's first in the shower?"

He wasn't suggesting they shower together, she noticed. "You go first."

Lying in the tumbled sheets, Kelsey watched him cross the room, the tall dark-haired man who'd brought her felicity beyond imagining. The bathroom door closed behind him.

Ridiculous that the bed should feel suddenly empty, or herself bereft. But if there was one thing she'd honed over the last ten years, it was an intuitive sixth sense that alerted her to emotions hidden below the surface. Luke, unless she was badly mistaken, had almost resented that last, unbearably sweet lovemaking.

She was borrowing trouble, Kelsey decided stoutly, and remembered Sister Elfreda. It was a glorious day, she was going to meet an artist she revered, and tonight, surely, she'd sleep in Luke's arms again.

What more could any woman ask?

RICO ALBENIZ, FOR all his fame, was a short, dumpy man with grizzled hair and boundless enthusiasm. He marched Kelsey into the rainforest at the island's southern tip, set up a canvas and told her to paint. The myriad greens, layered with sunlight, the riotous tropical blooms, were too new, too intense; as her brush stumbled and faltered, Rico plunged into the role of teacher. Gradually her palette became more adventurous, her strokes more confident. Deeply excited, she took greater risks, and all day absorbed everything he told her, doing her best to put it into practise.

At three o'clock, he announced, "Good. Very good. We will stop now, it's long past siesta. Tomorrow we will find waves on the beach and see how you paint light through water."

Kelsey rubbed her back, which she'd only now realized was on fire with tiredness. "Thank you, Rico. More than I can say."

"My good friend Luke said you had talent. He was right." Rico bowed from the waist. "The pleasure was mine."

Rico meant it, she thought humbly, following him out into the blinding sunshine, her head whirling. Back in her room, she fell onto the bed and slept for a solid two and a half hours.

When she woke, there was a message on her phone, advising her that she was to join Luke and Rico for dinner in the resort's main dining room. There'd be no intimate twosome with Luke, she realized.

As though her day outdoors and her long sleep had restored a measure of common sense, Kelsey took her thinking a step further. Last night Luke had seduced more than her body, for the intimacy he'd offered had gone far beyond the physical. He'd been generous, passionate and caring. He'd encouraged her to ask for what she wanted and to give what she longed to give. Could that be reduced to a little word like sex? Surely not.

Caution was what she'd better cultivate. She didn't want to get involved with anyone right now. She couldn't afford to. Her hard-earned freedom and her application to art school both beckoned with all the pent-up energy of the last ten years. If Rico Albeniz thought she was talented, she must be, she thought with an inward quiver of pure excitement. No one must get in the way of honing that talent.

Not even Luke.

Tall, dark, handsome, sexy Luke.

Dinner *à trois* was a fine idea. Although there was no reason why she shouldn't look her best.

To achieve that look took Kelsey longer than she'd expected. So she was late entering the dining room, which was banked with exquisite orchids and on three sides open to the dazzle of stars and the surf's pale murmur. Heads turned, she noticed with amusement, and confidently threaded her way toward the table where Luke and Rico were already seated.

She was wearing her slim silk skirt with a halter top, the matching loose jacket flung carelessly over one shoulder. Her hair was gathered in a soft knot of curls at the back of her head, baring the long line of her throat where the gold collar gleamed; her stiletto heels clicked softly on the parquet floor.

To her immense satisfaction, Luke's eyes narrowed when he saw her, his body still as a hunter's when he sights his prey. He stood up, kissed her formally on both cheeks, and held out her chair for her. Feeling like a princess, Kelsey said, "Thank you. Hello, Rico…"

She was going to enjoy every minute of the evening, she decided, accepting Luke's offer of wine, and was unsurprised when two hours later Rico tactfully left them in the resort's foyer and Luke said, "Let's go back to the villa."

"As long as I can take off these shoes and walk on the grass. They may be sexy, but they're killers."

Resting one hand on his sleeve, she bent to slip them off her feet. "Very sexy," Luke said, his voice thickening.

Again she felt that flare of purely feminine power. "Your place or mine?" she said, with a wicked smile.

"Mine, tonight."

His suite was in the opposite wing to hers, the walls a pale creamy yellow, the woodwork polished teak. Austere and minimal, Kelsey thought, looking around; no clues to the man whose temporary home it was, no photos, no knickknacks. "This room could belong to anyone," she said.

"Suits me that way."

"I know almost nothing about you."

"That suits me, too." His jaw tightened. "Although there's something you should know—I never take a woman to bed unless I use protection. But last night I did. Not just once—four times."

He could hear the anger in his voice. Was it against her, for being so unbearably seductive that he'd forgotten his own rule? Or against himself for being so easily seduced?

Long ago, he'd decided he'd never father a child.

With the same harshness, he added, "I'm assuming you're not on the pill."

"No, I'm not," she said evenly. "But several years ago, when I was having difficulty with my periods, I was told by a specialist that I may not be able to conceive. Or at least not easily. So I don't think you have to worry."

He gazed at her in silence. Why wasn't relief uppermost in his mind? "That must have been difficult for you to hear."

"Yes," Kelsey said, grateful for his understanding. "I'd

always envisaged having children some day. But if it's not meant to be…"

"We'll use protection from now on, just the same."

She voiced the question that had been hovering in her mind ever since she woke up. "Why did you come back to my room yesterday, Luke?"

"To tell you I was leaving the island this morning." He shrugged. "Then I heard you crying, and the rest you know."

"Are you sorry you didn't leave?" she blurted, her throat tight.

"It might have been smarter. Wiser. More prudent. But no, I'm not sorry." He reached out for her. "Enough talk—come here."

She knew that tone in his voice, and willingly walked into his embrace. But before his mouth plummeted to hers, she made herself a promise. After they'd made love, she was going to find out more about him, this man who'd burst into her safe little world and totally disrupted it. How could she sleep with someone she scarcely knew?

Then she forgot everything but the scorch of his lips on hers, and the desperate need to be naked in his arms. She heard Luke mutter, "Since the last time—since this morning—it feels like forever." Then nothing more was said by either of them, until she was indeed lying naked in his arms, utterly satiated, in that delicious lethargy that was the aftermath of storm.

"That was slower," he said lazily. "Maybe."

She chuckled. "Who's counting?"

"I can't get enough of you," he rasped, and again she heard an undertone of what was surely resentment.

She said casually, "Okay, Luke, I want to know your favorite antipasto and classic movie star."

He propped his head on one hand, smiling down at her. "*Prosciutto* rolls and Humphrey Bogart."

"Hmm. Mushroom *crostini* and Katharine Hepburn."

"So the relationship's over?" He tweaked a strand of her hair. "Favorite opera—*Don Carlos*."

"La Traviata."

"Favorite color—blue."

She grinned. "Azure, indigo or cerulean?"

"Should have realized an artist would complicate matters."

"Middle name?"

"Don't have one."

"Pauline," Kelsey said gloomily. "Who was your father?"

"Neatly done," Luke said softly. "But no cigar."

"Is your mother still alive?"

"Some things I don't talk about to anyone, Kelsey. Take it or leave it—because that's the way it is."

She said, in a conversational tone of voice, "I brought up three boys. It was bad enough when they tipped over Syd Crawley's outhouse on Hallowe'en, and broke two windows at school playing softball when they should have been in math class. Much worse when they realized fifty-one percent of the population was female." She traced the jut of Luke's cheekbone with her fingertip. "I'm very good at worming secrets out of guys."

"And I'm very good at keeping them."

"Then we'll see who wins."

Overturned outhouses and broken windows were kids' pranks compared to some of the things *he'd* done. "Yeah," he said, "we'll see. In the meantime, Kelsey Pauline North, I have this ambition to make very leisurely love to you. How about it?"

"I have an ambition, too—to seduce you," she said demurely. "Who goes first?"

Purposely, wanting to hear her delightful laugh again, he said, "Me. I'm the man."

In a flurry of limbs, she straddled him. "We could combine them. Me seducing you, slowly."

"Sounds like a plan," Luke said thickly. As she bent to kiss him, her hair enveloped him in silky waves of scent.

Seduced? he thought. Definitely.

CHAPTER SEVEN

WORKING IN WATERCOLORS, Kelsey spent three intense hours the next morning trying to capture the ebb and flow of the tides and the sparkle of light on the sea. Because their time together was limited, Rico was pushing her as hard as he dared. But she was all too willing to be pushed.

"Enough," he said finally. "I brought a picnic lunch, which we will enjoy here on the beach."

She was quaffing cold ginger beer when Rico said calmly, "I have been watching Luke. He's very attracted to you."

Some of the beer went down the wrong way. Choking, Kelsey gasped, "He's attracted to lots of women."

"He likes women. That's not what I mean. This—it's like the difference between a pale carmine wash and pigment straight from the tube."

Her heart was beating faster than she liked. "He won't tell me anything about his past, Rico."

"His childhood was very difficult." Rico shrugged, choosing a slice of mango. "He could easily have ended up in jail by the time he was fourteen. It's a credit to his character, his strength, that he didn't—and that he's achieved so much."

"Jail?" she whispered. "At fourteen?"

"Already I have said too much. Please, help me eat this delicious pineapple."

More questions, Kelsey thought in despair. The longer she spent with Luke, the greater an enigma he became. She said carefully, "You really like him, though?"

"I would trust him with my life."

Enigma, mystery. Did it matter how she described Luke? The intimacies he'd taken with her body only emphasized his inner seclusion.

She ate a chicken pastry in silence, painted her heart out for another hour, then walked back to the villa with Rico. There was no sign of Luke. Suddenly lonely beyond belief, she picked up the phone in her room and dialed Dwayne's number. He answered on the third ring. "Hi," she said, "how are you doing?"

"Hey, sis. Aced a physiology quiz, muddled my way through the anatomy of the ankle. Did you know…" And he was off.

Kelsey listened, amused by the passion in his voice. He'd make a wonderful doctor; certainly he should be able to fix a broken ankle.

Finally he said, "You could take the next quiz for me—I sure gave you the rundown. What's up with you?"

Trying to sound natural, she said, "I'm on vacation."

"'Bout time. Where?"

"A little island in the Bahamas." Quickly she described the job she'd done for Luke. "So I've paid my deposit to art school and I had some money left over."

"You on your own?"

"No," she said, overly casual. "Actually, I'm with Luke. It's his resort."

Dwayne's exaggerated whistle nearly split her eardrum. "Flying high, Kelse. I've read about him. Makes money as easy as picking apples and dumps women like they're the rotten ones in the barrel."

She said coolly, "Then maybe I'll dump him first."

"Been in the sack with him?"

"Yes. Don't you dare tell your younger brothers."

"Past time you had a good fling…you missed out on a lot by bringing the three of us up. But he better be good to you. He's not married, is he? Have you met his family? How old is he?"

With a clutch at her heart, she realized she didn't know how old Luke was. "He's a diversion, Dwayne," she said. "I don't need to know his family history."

"So you don't know much about him? You be careful, sis. He's one powerful guy—way out of your league. Don't let him mess you around."

"I'm going to art school, and ten Luke Griffins aren't going to stop me. Plus I'm going to live in my own place, without a hockey stick or a soccer ball in sight."

Dwayne laughed. "I'll leave my cleats behind when I come to visit. Guess I better get off the soapbox, seeing as how you're over the age of consent. Have a great time, and don't go falling in love with him."

"Not a chance. Let me give you a phone number where I can be reached." She reeled off the numbers. "Now I'm going for a swim in the pool…then I might order a rum punch with papaya and strawberries floating in it."

"A woman's gotta do what a woman's gotta do."

It was her turn to laugh. "Watch those anklebones. Love you, Dwayne."

"Love ya too."

She put down the phone. Although Dwayne took his position as the eldest of the three brothers seriously, he didn't have a worry in the world. She knew better than to fall in love with Luke Griffin. Dwayne was right: Luke was out of her league.

She might as well enjoy his luxurious villa while she was here, though. Her swim relaxed her; the rum punch was afloat with fruit. Afterward, she wandered up to the resort, wearing a sarong and white linen shirt over her bikini. But Luke, she discovered from the receptionist, had left the island this morning on business; he was expected back early this evening, and would meet her in the dining room at eight.

He hadn't bothered to tell her he was going away.

Why would he? she thought in a sudden surge of anger. She was just his mistress. There when he needed her, otherwise to be discounted. His work, his past, the things that mattered to him: they were nothing to do with her.

But beneath the anger lay pain. Somehow over the past few days she'd given Luke the power to hurt her.

Bad move, Kelsey.

She left the villa, strolling along the beach, and gradually the sheer beauty of Luke's retreat soothed her unease. The sea was a brilliant turquoise, with waves breaking on the coral reef; tall palms sliced the sand with their shadows. Wishing she'd brought her paints, she began collecting shells and fragments of coral, cupping them in a fold of her sarong, humming to herself.

Half an hour later, she slathered on more sunscreen, slipped out of her sarong and walked into the water. Closing her eyes against the sun's glare, she floated on her back and let her mind drift...

"You look like a water nymph."

Her eyes flew open. In a swirl of ripples she stood up. Luke was splashing toward her; his shadow fell across her body. "You got back," she said.

"An hour ago."

"I found out you were gone from the receptionist. Made me feel about two inches tall."

"I knew I'd be back before evening. It was nothing to do with you."

"Don't treat me as though I don't exist!"

"Is that what I do when we're in bed together?"

He was wearing the briefest of swim trunks. Tall, lean,

muscular, male to her female...liquid heat filled her belly. "No," she said shortly. "It's the rest of the time I'm talking about."

"Those were the terms."

"The terms were no commitment," she retorted. "But while we're together I expect to be informed of your whereabouts. By you."

"You look magnificent when you're angry," he said softly. Water swirling around his thighs, he seized her in his arms, clasping her by the hips. Bending his head, he kissed her sun warmed lips, her salty skin, and was instantly hard, drenched in need, his heart hammering in his ribcage.

Kelsey pounded on his chest with her fists and wrenched her head back. "I'm not through with the argument!"

"If I leave the island again, I'll tell you before I go. You pack a mean punch, lady."

"How else am I supposed to get through to you?"

If only he didn't like her so much, Luke thought, grinning into her furious face. "You haven't figured that out yet?" he said. "Where have you been the last couple of days?" Lifting her hand, he placed it on the most vulnerable part of his anatomy. "Now that's trust," he said.

Desire streaking her veins, Kelsey scowled at him. "Or stupidity."

His eyes danced with laughter. "I like my version better." In one swift movement he picked her up and waded through the shallows until his feet hit dry sand. Then he carried her further up the beach into the shadow of the palm fronds, where a few minutes ago he'd spread a blanket on the sand. "We've never made love outdoors," he said, and laid her down on her back.

Her heart was like a trip hammer in her breast. Eyes fastened to his, Kelsey unclasped her top and tossed it to one side, then eased her hips free of the tiny scrap of fabric that encircled them. Naked, she opened her arms to him.

He stripped off his suit. Dipping to cover her, his mouth seared hers. Branding her, she thought distantly.

He didn't need to.

His kisses streaked her body with fire and his hands laid claim to her until she was consumed by him. Then he lifted her to straddle him. She took him in and began to ride, head thrown back, her cries wild as a seabird's.

She broke, even as he broke within her.

Panting, she collapsed onto his bare chest, which was sheened with sweat. To her ears came the soft murmur of the sea, elemental as Luke's lovemaking. She was one with him, part of him, deeply connected…this man whom she scarcely knew.

When she found her voice, she muttered, "You'd have to file that one under I for intimacy."

"Nope. T for torrid," he said.

He was laughing at her again. Her head reared up. "Luke, neither of us wants this kind of intimacy. But let's not deny it exists—that's insulting to both of us."

"You go straight for the jugular, don't you?"

"Is there any other way?"

"It's sex that's between us, Kelsey. Incredible sex. Blow-my-mind-away sex—beyond anything in my experience. But let's not call it intimacy."

"I'll call it what I want."

"Sometimes I pity your three brothers."

"You don't need to—they could more than hold their own. And not one of them was afraid to be real."

"Goddammit, are you saying what we just did wasn't *real*?"

"I'm saying I'm more than my body, and so are you."

No, he wasn't, he thought grimly. Not when it came to women. "As I keep repeating, to the point of boredom, we set out the terms before we started."

"I told you, I'm not looking for commitment. I'm looking for honesty."

With reluctant admiration Luke said, "I'll tell you one thing—you're a mean fighter."

"I've had to fight. I bet you have, too."

No takers. His background was strictly off-limits. "All right," he grated, "I'll admit it—you're different from all my other women. But it's still just chemistry. Lust. I'm not going to call it anything else or let it get out of hand."

"It already is."

Wasn't every cell in his body crying out that she was right? "If it is," he said in a hard voice, "then it's just as well you're leaving the island in a few days."

Art school and a place of her own. Those were the priorities. Hold that thought, Kelsey, and don't let him get to you. Tossing her wet hair, she said, "Memories—is that all we want from each other?"

"To hell with memories," Luke said, his blue eyes blazing. "Right here, right now, I want to touch you, give you all the gifts of my body and please you to the best of my ability. That's major, Kelsey."

Sudden tears pricked at the backs of her eyes. "Yes," she said. "Yes, it is."

She drew him into her arms, holding his heat, his strength, knowing that, no matter what happened or what he said, he was already imprinted, unforgettably, on her memory.

THE SLOW DAYS passed. Rico left the island. Luke delegated as much of his work as he could to clear time to spend with Kelsey; he knew that when he did work, she was spending the time painting. He introduced her to windsurfing, snorkeling and sailing. They beachcombed, sampled all the dishes on the menu, swam in the ocean and the pool. And everything they did was punctuated by lovemaking. Fierce, frantic, sensual, laced with laughter... She had, he thought, as many moods as the sea.

He didn't look ahead, to when this magical interlude would come to an end. He didn't want to. But subliminally he was always aware of it.

Lying in bed with her early one morning, in a tumble of sheets, he lazily traced the curve of her cheekbone, as well known to him by now as his own face. "I'm hosting a dance and midnight buffet the day after tomorrow, for a CEOs' convention. Stay an extra day, Kelsey, and go with me."

Her lashes fell to hide her eyes. "I should go back... I have my first interview at the art school at the end of the week, and I've got to put the house on the market."

"One more day. The jet will take you home."

"I don't have an evening gown."

"Buy one at the boutique in the resort. Don't you want to go?"

She wanted to with a desperation that frightened her. Didn't it mean Luke was willing to go public with her? Introduce her to friends and business acquaintances?

So what? she thought unhappily. He'd gone public with a great many women over the years; she'd be just one more. The sooner she left, the better. Her body was in thrall to him, that had been obvious from the beginning. It was the rest of her she was worried about.

"I guess I could stay," she said.

I guess... Not good enough, Luke thought. "Promise?" he said, feeling his throat tighten; it was a word he usually avoided like the plague.

"Sure, I promise," she said lightly. "It'll be another chance to flaunt my lovely gold jewelry."

"Promises matter," he said harshly, and heard the words echo in his head. What in God's name had caused him to say them?

Kelsey was looking understandably puzzled. "It's okay," she said, "I'll go with you—I said I would."

He surged out of bed. "Good. Why don't we go windsurfing? Around eleven-thirty?"

She could spend the morning trying to paint the waxy pink orchids that flourished below her bedroom window. How lucky she was, Kelsey thought, and wished she could ask Luke what that little interchange had been about.

No Trespassing. That was the name of Luke Griffin's game.

ON THE DAY of the dance, Kelsey spent the afternoon at the spa. Back in her room, she had a light supper to tide her over. Then she bathed, wallowing in bubble bath and warbling her way through her favorite musicals. Finally she put on her new evening gown and gold sandals, fastened her jewelry and walked over to the mirror.

For a moment she was lost in wonderment that the tall, elegant woman in the slender sheath of dark green silk was herself. Her hair had been drawn back from her face, a few loose strands artfully teasing her cheeks; the exotically shaped dark eyes and full lips surely didn't belong to her?

How would she go back to being ordinary Kelsey North?

She'd worry about that tomorrow, she thought, and with a surge of excitement heard Luke tap on her door. Swaying on her high heels, she let him in.

His tux and formal shirt gave him an air of formidable sophistication, yet more than hinted at the virile male body beneath. He moved as gracefully, as lethally, as a jaguar, she thought, and struggled to sound casual. "You look very handsome."

"You're like a flower," he said huskily. "Long-stemmed, your hair the color of chrysanthemums. Come here, Kelsey."

Without a moment's hesitation she walked into his arms. She smelled subtly of flowers, he realized, a layered perfume that suited her complexity; her body was pliant as a stem in the wind.

She was leaving tomorrow. How would he manage without her?

He didn't have to, he thought, drinking deep of the sweetness of her mouth. His headquarters were in Manhattan. Her art school was in Manhattan. Bingo.

He wasn't done with her yet.

"You'll be the sexiest woman in the room," he muttered, grazing her jawline with his teeth, nipping at her earlobe, hearing her breath quicken. No, he definitely wasn't done with her. How could he be, when all his senses went on high alert anytime he was within ten feet of her?

"We'd better stop," she said breathlessly, "or we'll never get there."

"Yeah," he said, and kissed her again, raw hunger ripping through his body. "Too bad I'm the host."

Shrill as an alarm, the telephone by her bed rang. Once, twice. With a muttered oath Luke released her. "It could be for me—answer it, would you, Kelsey?"

With fingers that weren't quite steady, she brushed a tendril of hair back from her flushed cheeks and hurried over to the phone. "Hello?"

"It's Dwayne—glad I caught you. Glen was in a car accident this evening, sis. He's going to be okay. But he's in the Massachusetts General and I thought I should let you know."

The color drained from Kelsey's face. Gripping the phone, her knuckles white, she blurted, "How did it happen? How badly is he hurt?"

"Wet snow followed by freezing rain—the roads were slick as glass and a half-ton collided with him. Broken ribs, bruising and concussion. They plan to keep him under observation until tomorrow."

"I'll come as soon as I can. Will you stay until I get there?"

"Sure, I squared it with my profs. Kirk's flying in as well. We'll have a North reunion."

How could he joke? "I'll call you on your cell once I've made arrangements. Thanks, Dwayne. Tell Glen I love him."

She put down the receiver. Her heart was thumping, her

belly cold as ice. It was terrifying how quickly things could change, she thought, and, turning, saw that Luke was watching her.

Was it her imagination that the distance between them seemed suddenly immense? Briefly, doing her best to keep her voice steady, she relayed what Dwayne had told her. "I have to go right away…is your jet available?"

"Take a deep breath," Luke ordered. "Then tell me why you're rushing off like this. Or am I missing something?"

"I just told you why!"

"Don't misunderstand me, Kelsey—I'm sorry your brother's been in an accident, and I'm really glad his injuries aren't severe. But that's the point…they aren't severe. So what's the panic?"

"He's in hospital. I have to go."

Keeping a tight hold on a depth of anger he didn't fully understand, Luke said, checking off his fingers, "He's not dying. He's not in ICU. He's not on the critical list. Am I right so far?"

"Yes," Kelsey said through gritted teeth. "You don't get it, do you? He's my brother. I need to—"

"Go tomorrow morning. You promised you'd go to the dance with me tonight."

"I know I did! But things have changed—I didn't know this was going to happen."

"You promised me," Luke said. "If you go, you're breaking that promise."

"For someone who has a fit if the word *commitment* is mentioned, you sure put a lot of weight on a promise."

"The minute one of your brothers calls, do you always drop everything and run?"

She said faintly, "You're jealous."

Luke took her by the arm, his fingers digging into her flesh. "Don't be trivial. I figured I could depend on you, Kelsey. I would have taken that to the bank. But I guess I was wrong."

She made one last try. "I need to see for myself that Glen's all right. They're my family, Luke, the only family I have."

"And what am I?"

She said with painful accuracy, "You're the man I've slept with the last eight days."

His eyes were like chips of ice. "Aren't you forgetting the nights?"

"Will you or won't you put your jet at my disposal?"

"That was the deal. I, at least, won't go back on my word."

She flinched; hadn't she kept her word for ten long years, under circumstances that had trapped and confined her? "I guess you didn't have much of a family life, Luke," she said evenly, "but even so, I thought you'd understand."

She was abandoning him, Luke thought, his gut clenched. Breaking her promise. As though a wave had burst over his head, he was suddenly inundated with all his mother's promises, every one of them broken as though they'd meant nothing.

"I'll talk to the pilot right away," he said, and strode over to the phone and made the call. Putting down the receiver, he said in a clipped voice, "He'll be ready to leave in just under an hour."

"If I'd gone back today, the way I planned, you'd have attended the dance on your own."

"That's what I'll do now." The words were out before he could stop them. "Although I may not *stay* on my own."

Stabbed to the heart, Kelsey said bitterly, "The disposable woman. That's me."

All his women were disposable. Sooner or later. "You're not in love with me?" he said sharply.

"Of course not," she answered with matching sharpness. "I just don't understand why you don't get it—about Glen, I mean. How could I sit and make small talk all night when my brother's in hospital?"

The little break in her voice almost undid him. Hardening his heart, Luke said, "I have to go, they're expecting me. Goodbye, Kelsey."

If he kissed her, he'd be lost.

"Goodbye," she said, with utter finality.

Turning on his heel, Luke marched out the door and along the hallway. The pool shimmered in the moonlight. He walked faster. He'd allowed Kelsey to get too close to him. Much too close. He was starting to need her, for God's sake.

His bed would be a wasteland tonight without her.

It didn't have to be. Clarisse's name had turned up on the guest list. She was accompanied by her father, a steel magnate.

Outside, the crushed shells on the path crunched under his black shoes. The resort was brightly lit, music drifting to his ears. He was the host; he had to go and act the part.

Was he making the biggest mistake of his life, to let Kelsey slip through his fingers for the sake of a promise?

Schooling his features to impassivity, Luke strode toward the foyer.

WHEN KELSEY WALKED into the hospital room, Kirk gave a rude whistle and Dwayne's jaw dropped. She was wearing the tangerine coat and cashmere dress Luke had given her; her leather boots tapped on the floor.

Glen said weakly, "You should go away more often, sis—you look great."

She bent to kiss him, her eyes filmed with tears. "You scared me worse last night than the day you fell out of the oak tree. Nine years ago, that was."

"How was I to know the rope'd break?" he said. "Insurance will cover the car, and they're springing me loose from here later on today."

Kirk said, eyeing his sister, "Fancy duds. But it's not just that. You look different."

Glen said, "She got laid. That's the difference."

She said vigorously, "We are *not* entering into a discussion of my sex-life."

"So where is he?" Dwayne asked. "We gotta meet him."

"He didn't come."

"He let you travel all this way on your own?"

"In his private jet and a rented limo," she said dryly.

Kirk interjected, "You dating him after you go to art school?"

Summoning all her aplomb, she replied with admirable coolness, "I doubt it. It was a fling, guys. Short and sweet. Now it's over, and I'd really prefer to change the subject."

"The guy's a jerk," Dwayne said trenchantly.

"You don't look very happy," Kirk added.

"The whole way up I was worried sick about your brother," she said evasively. "But there was all this food on the plane, so I stole some. I hope your appetites haven't shrunk since you left home."

Flaky croissants with crabmeat filling, brioche and an assortment of cheeses succeeded in changing the subject from Luke. She didn't want to talk about Luke. Now or ever.

This resolve lasted until she was at the airport that evening. Glen was recuperating in his apartment, planning to catch up on coursework online, Kirk was flying back to forestry school, and Dwayne was going to take a cab back to the residence.

He was flicking through a discarded copy of a newspaper as they waited for Kirk's flight to be called. Suddenly his hands stilled. "Luke Griffin—he's the guy who whisked you off to the Bahamas?"

Kelsey nodded, training her face to immobility. He passed her the paper. "Doesn't look like he's missing you any."

It was the society page. The photo, in color, leaped out at her. Luke was in his tux in the resort's ballroom, smiling down at a cool, elegant blond who was poured into a silver lamé dress. Her hand was resting on his sleeve, her body curving into his in unmistakable invitation. "'Clarisse Andover, who flew in from Paris, enjoying the company of her host, Luke Griffin,'" she read, the words blurring in her vision.

I may not stay on my own…

He hadn't, she thought sickly. Not even for one night.

"I knew his reputation before I went," she mumbled.

"Son of a bitch," Dwayne said.

Of the three brothers, Dwayne was the one least likely to swear. "I'm well rid of him," Kelsey said, trying to sound as though she meant it. "I guess one of his tricks is to treat each woman he's with as though she's the best thing that ever happened to him. I kind of fell for that. Silly me."

"Bastard," Kirk snarled.

With a surge of relief Kelsey heard the flight announcement. Ten minutes later she was waving goodbye to Dwayne, whose last words had been, "Call me if you need a shoulder to cry on."

She did. Right now. Because Luke's callous replacement of her had torn her to shreds.

No commitment didn't begin to cover it.

CHAPTER EIGHT

LUKE SLAMMED THE door to his penthouse and yanked off his tie. Flinging it over the leather chesterfield, he tossed his jacket after it. It was time he made a list.

No more dates with Liz, who'd sent a perfectly good meal back to the kitchen because the decorative rosemary sprig was wilted.

No more dates with Marlene, who'd both simpered and tittered for four excruciatingly long hours. Simpering was bad enough. Reacting to everything he said with a silly little giggle was enough to drive a man to drink.

No more dates with Ursula, Manhattan's latest supermodel, who'd spent the whole evening in a pose of—admittedly beautiful—boredom, as though a photographer was about to take her picture. The faintest of smiles. Yes, she'd condescended to produce a couple of those. Just. But a laugh had been beneath her.

Why didn't he quit dating altogether? Perhaps his temper would improve.

So was he into making lists now, like Kelsey? Kelsey had loved every meal that had been put in front of her because she hadn't had to cook it. Kelsey, he'd bet his bottom dollar, wouldn't know how to simper. But she sure knew how to laugh.

He missed her unrelentingly, in bed and out.

Numbers four, five and six on the list: quit thinking about Kelsey North and quit waking up at night reaching for her, then bellyaching because she wasn't there.

He hadn't replaced her in that bed. Hadn't had the slightest urge to.

Women, he thought savagely. They either irritated the hell out of a guy, or else they wormed their way through his defenses and made themselves indispensable.

It was exactly nine weeks since Kelsey had left the island. Not that he was counting.

The day after her departure he'd phoned the hospital in Boston and been told that Glen North had already been discharged.

So there'd been no need for her to break her promise.

Her house had been sold; he'd found that out later on, by a couple of judicious phone calls. She'd also been accepted at art school. Neither of those events had caused her to phone him.

She hadn't made a single attempt to get in touch with him.

Was that why he was in such a foul mood? He was used to women chasing him. It was as plain as the simper on Marlene's face that Kelsey had lost interest in him the minute her brother had phoned. He hated admitting it, but his pride was hurt. After all that incredible sex, she could simply turn her back on him? Sell her house, apply to art school, get on with her life?

Be damned if he was going to crawl, or beg for her attention. He was through with her. Finished.

He jammed his hands in his pockets. In all fairness, Kelsey couldn't have understood the import of the promise she'd made about going to the dance. The reason was simple: he'd never told her anything about his mother's string of broken promises, and the pain—physical and emotional—they'd caused him as a little boy. He'd kept his mouth tight shut. So for Kelsey the trip to Boston had been a simple choice between a temporary lover and a much-loved brother.

Could he blame her for making that choice?

Maybe, he thought with a nasty tightening of his nerves, she'd seen the photo in the society pages of him and Clarisse at the ball on the island. When he'd come across it the next day he'd been both appalled and infuriated. Had he actually *smiled* at Clarisse as she'd clung to him like a tick to a dog?

Surely Kelsey hadn't seen it? What reason would she have to read the society pages? Although it would explain her silence if she had.

Luke heaved an exasperated sigh. He was looking for excuses; he didn't want to admit that she'd simply turned her back on him because she'd had enough of him. Because she could cross travel, painting and torrid sex off her list. Mission accomplished.

He was well rid of her, he thought, gazing through his bank of tall windows with their spectacular view of the bare-limbed trees of Central Park and the myriad lights of the city.

Why the devil did the art school have to be in Manhattan, practically on his own front door?

Restlessly Luke wandered into the huge kitchen, that he used as rarely as possible, and took a beer out of the stainless steel refrigerator. Uncapping it, he let the cool liquid slide down his throat. First he'd been determined to have Kelsey, and now he was equally determined to stay away from her. What kind of man did that make him? Indecisive? Manipulative? Confused?

No, he thought. Deep down he'd known Kelsey would upset the life he'd so carefully constructed, with its clever system of checks and balances. So he'd sent her away, washing his hands of her. Tough, hardheaded and decisive. That was a more accurate description.

He didn't want Kelsey North any more than he wanted Liz, Marlene or Ursula.

He'd go and lift weights for an hour. Who needed sex?

* * *

NINE WEEKS AFTER Kelsey had left the Bahamas to see Glen, she spent her first night in the bachelor apartment in Manhattan that she was renting at exorbitant cost. Bachelor closet, more like, she thought, lying wide awake as the people next door hiked their stereo up another notch and a siren howled on the street five floors below.

She was tired and needed her sleep. She was also desperately, horribly homesick. She missed her house and her brothers and her unexciting life in Hadley; she even missed Alice the postmistress.

But at least she didn't miss Luke. Insensitive, controlling, unfaithful Luke.

With a sigh Kelsey turned over in bed, pummeling the pillow. She'd sold the house and most of the furniture. Her final interview at art school was the day after tomorrow. She'd been accepted; she already knew that. This interview took the form of a critique of the portfolio she'd sweated over for weeks.

She was committed. No going back.

She did miss Luke, missed him horribly; she'd be lying if she pretended otherwise. And the nights were the worst.

Sex, she thought fiercely, that was what she missed. Not him. But if that was true, why had her brief rebellion against village mores and her own constricted life resulted in a loneliness greater than any she'd ever known?

Luke's continued silence was a huge part of that loneliness. Hadn't they laughed together, swum and played together, argued about politics and the toppings for a perfect pizza? He'd become, even in those few days, a friend. Or so she'd thought.

But then Dwayne had called and Luke had stripped her of any illusions of friendship. Or even common decency.

Kelsey pulled a pillow over her head and started listing all the contents of her paintbox. Eventually she fell asleep.

* * *

KELSEY WOKE EARLY, to the blare of horns and the roar of traffic. In Hadley she woke up to birdcalls overlying the distant murmur of the sea. Oh, God, was she going to be able to do this? Live in one of the biggest cities in the world, expose her fledgling talents in a prestigious art school, all on her own?

Curled in a ball, she hugged her belly. She didn't feel so hot. In fact, she felt lousy. In sudden alarm she reared up from the bed and fled to the tiny bathroom, where she fell to her knees and threw up into the toilet.

Oh, great. The flu. That was all she needed.

Carefully Kelsey stood up, rinsed her face and cleaned her teeth. She was as white as a ghost. But she felt minimally better. When she thought back, she'd been nauseous the last couple of days; she must have been coming down with some kind of bug.

She pulled open the medicine cabinet over the sink, looking for mouthwash, which for some reason she'd stashed next to her tampons.

In a flood of sheer terror she stared at the pink and white box. She'd just been sick. In the morning. How long since she'd had a period?

Quickly she cast back. Not since going to the island, she realized in another surge of panic. She'd been so busy, so distracted with lists and deadlines that she hadn't even noticed its absence.

She and Luke hadn't used any protection that first night they'd spent together. In good faith she'd assured him it was unlikely she'd get pregnant.

She couldn't be pregnant. No way.

Last week she'd noticed her breasts were fuller, tender to the touch. For the last three weeks she'd been exhausted to the point of dizziness.

Overtiredness, that was all. She'd accomplished more in the last nine weeks than most women could do in four months.

Put that together with the stress of Luke's defection, and she had a perfect recipe for her cycle to be disrupted.

Like a woman acting out a script she hadn't had the time to rehearse, Kelsey searched among some papers on her desk and found the name of the walk-in clinic nearest her. She got there by ten in the morning, saw a doctor at eleven-thirty, and was walking back to her apartment fifteen minutes later.

She *was* pregnant. With Luke Griffin's child. Her hands were as cold as ice, while her heart was fluttering in her chest like a trapped and panic-stricken bird.

But, to her consternation, every now and then the bird would escape its cage in a burst of joyous wings. Miraculously, she, Kelsey North, had conceived a child. Her very own child.

Then terror would again usurp joy. Pregnant? She couldn't be! Pregnancy for sure wasn't on her list.

The elevator in the apartment building was out of order. She tramped up four flights of stairs and unlocked her door, latching it tight shut behind her. The little space seemed for the first time like a haven.

Pregnant.

Would she tell them at the art school? How would she break the news to her brothers? Then how would she prevent them from chasing Luke with a shotgun?

Could she manage to bring up a baby on her own? What would happen once her money ran out?

She should never have sold the house, she thought in another surge of terror. She couldn't bring up a child in a dumpy apartment block in Manhattan, where there wasn't a tree in sight, let alone a sea breeze riffling the leaves.

Luke. Father of her child.

Kelsey sat down hard on the bed, gazing unseeingly at the poster she'd tacked to the opposite wall. A poster of Tuscany, a place she'd always longed to visit.

Luke had had, according to Rico, a very difficult childhood.

Didn't he deserve to be told he'd fathered a child of his own? Surely he'd want to play his part in bringing up that child?

Kelsey groaned aloud. She'd been criminally stupid not to have thought of protection. But Luke, who was so much more experienced, hadn't thought of it either; she wasn't the only one responsible for this mess.

If he insisted on being involved with the child she was carrying, she'd be bound to him for years.

Luke Griffin, with his sophisticated women and his platinum credit cards? He wouldn't want anything to do with a baby. A baby was much too real.

She couldn't in good conscience keep the choice from him, though. He had to be told.

Her interview at the art school was tomorrow afternoon. She'd phone his office afterward and see if he was there; she could meet him in a restaurant nearby, on neutral territory.

Get it over with.

In another wash of panic, Kelsey buried her head in her hands.

LATE THE FOLLOWING afternoon Kelsey was marching down the granite steps of the art school, her face set. Her critique had been exhaustive and nerve-racking, but ultimately affirming. It had been Professor Dougald with the red hair, the vague smile and the paint-spattered shirt, who'd burst her bubble. First he'd mentioned her sponsorship by Rico Albeniz. That was fine, she knew about it and felt she'd earned it. But then he'd mentioned that Luke Griffin had also sponsored her. Such a generous donor to the school, such beneficence.

Kelsey felt as though the bottom had dropped out of her world. She hadn't been accepted to the school solely on her own merits, as she'd assumed. Luke had stuck his oar in by donating a big wad of money. Money talked. Of course they hadn't turned her down.

How dared he? How did he have the gall to sponsor her as

an artist when he hadn't even waited twenty-four hours to replace her in his bed? Answers, she thought grimly, darting across the street like a seasoned New Yorker. She was going to get some answers. Right now.

Griffin Tower was an imposing pile of granite and glass, but Kelsey was in no mood to be impressed. She marched into the lobby and said to the receptionist, a glossy brunette, "Is Mr Griffin in?"

"I believe so. Do you have an appointment?"

"No. Tell him Kelsey North is here. He'll find time to see me, I'm sure."

The receptionist didn't even bat a tastefully painted eyelid. "One moment, please, Ms North." She picked up the phone, pushed an extension and said, "There's a Ms Kelsey North to see Mr Griffin. Would you check with him, please? He will? I'll send her up."

She smiled at Kelsey. "Take the left-hand elevator, it goes straight to Mr Griffin's floor. The receptionist there will show you the way to his office."

"Thank you," Kelsey said. He *would* have his own personal elevator, she thought viciously. No mixing with the ordinary folk for Luke Griffin.

The elevator was also glossy, all smoky mirrors and polished marble, and the ride so smooth she scarcely felt the motion. She was deposited in a hushed, carpeted hallway with a single stark abstract on the wall.

Luke's receptionist was blond. Surprise, surprise, Kelsey thought, and said crisply, "Kelsey North, to see Mr Griffin."

"Mr Griffin said for you to go right in. It's the last door down the hall, Ms North."

All the doors were discreetly closed. Luke's bore a simple brass plaque with his name. Not bothering to knock, Kelsey pushed the door open and walked in.

CHAPTER NINE

LUKE WAS SITTING behind an imposing antique desk, gazing at a computer screen. As Kelsey pulled the door smartly shut behind her, he clicked the mouse and got to his feet, smiling at her. "Kelsey," he said, "this is a nice surprise."

His blue shirt was open at the neck, the sleeves rolled up. With a pang of sheer lust, she remembered kissing the pulse at the base of his throat, stroking the corded muscles of his forearm. That she should still desire him, after all that had happened, only stoked her rage. She said choppily, "I just found out that you sponsored me at the art school by donating money to them. How dare you interfere in my life?"

Any thoughts Luke might have had about Kelsey coming here to resume their affair died a swift death. Furious with himself, he said coldly, "I've donated to them before. You're not the center of the universe."

Her anger rose another notch. "One of the professors told me about the donation and coupled it with my acceptance. So now I'll never know if I would have made the cut based solely on talent."

"Of course you would have. A school with that reputation? I could have donated a cool billion, and if you were a lousy artist they'd have turned you down."

"You had no right to sponsor me after the way you treated

me! Wanting me to go to a stupid dance when one of my brothers was in hospital. Not even trying to understand."

"He was released in less than twenty-four hours," Luke said unwisely. "I rest my case."

"How do you know when he was released?"

"One phone call was all it took."

Her voice was dangerously quiet. "Have you made any other phone calls about me?"

Be damned if he was going to lie. "I found out you sold the house."

"At least I know you didn't buy it—the price I got was too low."

Her cheekbones were stained scarlet; her eyes, those exotic dark pools, blazed with fury. Even her hair looked alive, sparking with electricity, shot through with copper. He still wanted her, Luke thought. Hungered for her, ached for her, lusted after her. That hadn't changed.

"So," she seethed, "you replace me in your bed when it's scarcely had the time to cool off, then you stalk me with phone calls. It's called harassment, Luke. Or isn't that word in your vocabulary?"

"I have yet to replace you in my bed," he said with total accuracy.

"You— *What* did you say?"

"You heard. I presume you saw the photo in the society pages, of me and Clarisse?"

Pain pierced the red mist of anger. "You're damn right I did. She looked like she couldn't wait to get you naked—and you smiling at her like she was the best thing since rum punch."

"I was in a fog that night, Kelsey. I didn't even see the photographer. Yeah, Clarisse and I were an item last year for a few months. But it's over and won't be reopened. I haven't slept with anyone since you left." His eyes bored into hers, blue as the sky. "I can't prove it. But it's true."

"I see," Kelsey said, as a weight she'd scarcely known she was carrying lifted from her shoulders. "Why not?"

He walked around the desk. "I made a list—it must be catching. *Quit dating* topped the list. Any woman I went out with either bored me to tears or irritated the hell out of me."

"You weren't just irritated with me the night I left, you were furious."

Tell it like it is, Luke. She deserves the truth. "My mother broke every promise she ever made to me. As a consequence, promises are hugely important to me." As instant comprehension flashed across Kelsey's face, he labored on, "But underneath it all I was getting in too deep with you. Breaking my own rules."

"You wanted sex. Not intimacy."

"Right on. When your brother phoned, he gave me the perfect excuse to end our affair. So I insisted you keep a promise whose import you didn't understand, and forced you to choose between me and Glen."

"Playing dirty."

"You did say you wanted freedom."

"I did… You're right. I still do." She added, thinking hard, "Someone like me wasn't in your game plan."

"Still isn't."

"So you dumped me as if I didn't even exist," Kelsey said, her voice threaded with remembered pain.

"No commitment. That was the deal."

"Then why did you sponsor me?" she flared.

"I talked to Rico after you left. He was so excited about your talent, and thought it essential you get into the best school. He wasn't sure his name would be enough, because he's better known in Europe and South America than here. So he wondered if I could add a little leverage." Luke shrugged. "I trust his judgment totally. The sale price for Griffin's Keep went straight to the school."

Kelsey wrinkled her nose. "That hideous old pile?"

He took another step closer, her flowery scent drifting to his nostrils, filling him with memories. "It seemed a nice symmetry that the place that brought us together should give you something you'd always wanted—art school." He hesitated. "This might sound arrogant as all get out, but I don't even have to ask if you've replaced me in your bed. You wouldn't do that quickly or casually."

"Actually," she said, "in between selling old sportsgear, cleaning the house top to bottom, dealing with real estate agents, putting together a portfolio and finding an apartment in Manhattan that wouldn't bankrupt me in a week, I had several all-night orgies."

"I don't think so." Luke's smile faded. "I'm not sure I can keep my hands off you."

He reached for her at the same moment she fell into his arms. Heaven, Kelsey thought, feeling his steel strength and the heat of his body sizzle along her nerves, tightening them to an unbearable pitch. Her veins were on fire. Her bones dissolved. As his mouth clamped to hers, she moaned deep in her throat. Consumed by him, steeped in him, she thrust with her tongue.

Pulling her to his erection, he scraped her lower lip with his teeth. "My bed's been like a desert without you," he said hoarsely. And knew those were words he'd never intended to say.

She was tugging at the buttons on his shirt, her fingers hot on his flesh, sliding over his ribcage and taut belly. Rediscovering, remembering, rejoicing… Then Luke kissed her again, ravaging her mouth, and she met him with her own fierce impatience.

He pushed her coat from her shoulders, yanking her sweater from her waistband. As the air struck her bare flesh, Kelsey gasped, "The door—"

"No one ever interrupts me in my office. They know better." Lust ripped through him as her hips writhed against his hardness. He pushed her backward, against the wall, tearing at the button on her pants, dragging the zipper down, cupping her mossy heat in his palm. As though his touch was all she'd been waiting for, she arched and peaked, stifling her whimpers in his chest.

He hauled her sweater over her head, desperate to feast his eyes on her. Her bra joined his shirt on the carpet. Her breasts, so firm and ripe, their tips like small stones...fuller than they used to be, he thought suddenly, for had he ever forgotten a single detail of her body? Swollen, the areolas darker...and her waistline, with that very slight thickening he'd noticed almost subconsciously, just before bringing her to climax...

He said, his voice coming from a long way away, "Kelsey, are you pregnant?"

She froze in his arms, desire eclipsed by naked fear. "Yes," she said.

"Am I the father?" Of course he was, he thought blankly. He was the man who'd taken her virginity.

She looked at him steadily. "Yes, the child's yours."

"When were you planning to tell me?"

"I only found out yesterday."

Anger licked along his veins. "Perhaps I should rephrase that— *Were* you planning to tell me?"

Her nostrils flared. "Of course I was! I'd decided I had to." Making a wild guess, she added, "You grew up without a father—am I right?"

"I never laid eyes on him. I don't even know who he was."

She bit her lip. "I wanted to give you the chance to play a role in your child's upbringing."

Pregnant, Luke thought. With his child. Was it really true? "In the Bahamas, you said you'd probably never be able to conceive."

"That's what I was told, and that's what I believed. Not that I would have thought of protection anyway. You didn't think of it either, Luke."

He hadn't. Not once. "So when were you planning to break the news?"

"Stop it!" she cried, leaning down to grab her bra and sweater, then pulling them on with fingers that felt as clumsy as a two-year-old's. "I believed you when you said you didn't go to bed with Clarisse—but you won't believe I had every intention of telling you about the baby? Keep your double standards, Luke Griffin. I don't want them."

"Pregnancy isn't on my list," he said in a hard voice.

"It wasn't on mine either."

"Is abortion?"

She paled. "No! It never occurred to me."

Something tight inside him relaxed. He should have known better than to ask, he thought slowly, and knew he'd uncovered another layer to the complexity that was Kelsey. "Do your brothers know?"

"Are you kidding?" She gave him a humorless smile. "You'd better watch your back when they find out."

"That bad, eh?"

"Oh, yes. Dwayne and Kirk both saw the photo of you and Clarisse—it was Dwayne who pointed it out to me at the airport. Gullible. That's what they think I am. A polite way of saying brainless."

She was fumbling with the button on her waistband. He bent to pick up his shirt, searching for a neutral topic, anything to settle a shock he still hadn't absorbed. "What are you going to do about art school?"

"I haven't had time to think things through yet. But the school operates on a semester system. I'll take the first two, then skip one when the baby's born."

"What about money?"

"I'll manage," she said sharply. "This isn't about money, Luke."

"Everything's about money."

"In your world, maybe. Not in mine." Then her eyes widened. Aghast, she blurted, "This baby isn't some kind of scheme to get my hands on the Griffin millions. Surely you don't believe that of me?"

He said slowly, "You shoot straight, Kelsey, not around corners."

"Oh." So he *did* understand some things about her, this enigmatic, guarded man. To her dismay her eyes were swimming with tears. "Well, that's good."

He brushed her wet lashes with his fingertip. "Don't cry. I can't stand it."

"Hormones," she said with a watery grin. "That's the other thing I've got to do. Buy a book about pregnancy. Then I'll take the next few days, before classes start, to do some heavy-duty planning. Figure out exactly how I'm going to handle this."

She wasn't saying *we,* she was saying *I,* he noticed with another flare of rage. "Where?"

"Where what?"

"Where are you going to do the planning?"

"In my apartment. My I-hate-to-tell-you-how-much-it-costs-per-square-inch bachelor apartment."

He shoved his shirt into his trousers and buckled his belt. "Let's go check it out."

"You want to see it? Now?"

"Now's as good a time as any." He held her coat out, easing it on her shoulders, tugging her hair free of the collar. Her sexy, tumbled hair. Unable to help himself, he bent to kiss her nape, and felt her shiver in response.

His own body's response was unmistakable. But could he make love to her? A woman who was pregnant with his child?

Was he out of his mind?

"Let's go," he said brusquely.

They traveled in Luke's chauffeured limo; the apartment block, even at dusk, looked depressingly dingy. Luke glanced around without comment, then followed Kelsey up the stairs because the elevator still hadn't been fixed. She unlocked the door and ushered him inside.

"Per square inch is right," Luke said, feeling his gut tighten with anger. As a little boy he'd lived in places like this. In worse places too. Much worse. He tried to picture Kelsey getting out of class late at night, walking streets that were only borderline safe, then tramping up the narrow stairwell, only to end up in a room you couldn't swing a cat in.

He'd never doubted her courage or determination: she had plenty of both. But if a mugger attacked a pregnant woman, courage and determination weren't always enough.

His resolve hardening, he glanced at the poster on the opposite wall; he knew exactly where it had been taken. "Why Tuscany?"

"I've always wanted to go there," she said briefly. "You've seen my place now, Luke. Once I'm done planning, I'll let you know what I've decided."

"Is that a hint for me to bow out gracefully? Walk down the stairs and leave you to figure things out all by yourself?"

"I'm tired, and for now we've said everything that needs saying."

"Oh, no, we haven't," he said softly. "You're leaving out one all-important factor—the child's father. Who might have some plans of his own."

She tensed. "Plans? What do you mean?"

"I'm not sure yet. Which is why you and I are going out for dinner. So we can talk."

"You don't get it—*I* have to make the decisions first. Then we'll talk."

"It took two of us to make this baby, and it'll take two of us to plan how to handle the situation. Grab your purse and let's go."

With a defiant lift of her chin, Kelsey unbuttoned her coat

and turned to toss it on the bed. But she turned too fast, and in a wave of dizziness stumbled against the wall. Luke was behind her in an instant, taking her in his arms, bringing her around to face him. Her cheeks were ashen pale. "For God's sake," he rasped, "how often does that happen?"

"It's only the fourth time," she mumbled, trying to clear the swirling in her head. "I just have to remember to take things slow."

His brain in overdrive, he said, "Is your overnight bag in the closet?"

Her head jerked up. "I don't need an overnight bag to go out for dinner."

"You let me decide what you need." He scooped her up in his arms and laid her on the narrow bed, pulling the throw at the foot of the bed over her legs. "And stay right there while I pack."

She pushed herself upright. "Stop taking over my life."

"Things have changed, Kelsey. There are three of us in the mix now." He pulled her suitcase out of the jammed closet. "You need an organizer," he said nastily, and took her sundresses off the hangers. Then he pulled open her bureau drawers, stuffing the case with underwear and finding her passport under her socks with a grunt of satisfaction. "That should do. Do you need to rest any longer or shall we go?"

"I'm not going back to the Bahamas!"

"I haven't asked you to." He took out his cellphone and spoke briefly into it. "We've got a reservation at Scranton's, ten blocks from here. Scarcely the Bahamas."

She rolled her eyes. "Nothing but the best."

"Life's short." He zipped up her case and said with a predatory grin, "I can carry this *and* you."

"You're like a steamroller," she fumed, "flattening everything in your path."

"It gets results."

Kelsey stood up, bracing herself against the wall. "Are you telling me I'm staying at your place tonight? Making love with you again?"

"Is that what you want to do?"

She let out her breath in an exasperated sigh. "Cute, Luke. Answer the question."

"We'll start with dinner at Scranton's."

"If sex is all that's on your mind, you should know by now you don't have to waste your money feeding me dinner."

"I'm hungry for something other than you—so we'll eat, plan, have sex. In that order."

She said flatly, "I'm not giving up art school. I've waited too long."

"No reason you should have to give it up."

She gave another exasperated sigh; some color had returned to her cheeks. "I wish, just for one minute, I could read your mind."

"X-rated."

"Huh. I'm going to eat my way down the menu and cost you a bundle." She grimaced. "But no wine. Seems like yesterday I was trying to persuade three teenagers to drink milk, and now I'm stuck with it."

"Scranton's will be happy to serve you milk in a wine glass, I'm sure."

Scranton's, Kelsey decided, five minutes after they were seated, would serve champagne in a soup bowl if Luke Griffin requested it. She ran her eyes down the menu. She'd probably lose most of this delectable food first thing in the morning, but never mind. Right now she was seated across from the sexiest man in the restaurant, whose sky-blue eyes made her melt in a puddle on the very expensive carpet.

Didn't she, with every fiber of her being, long to be in bed with him again? Naked in his arms, swept away by the sexual alchemy between them? Perhaps it was just as well he'd packed her overnight bag.

Pregnancy, at least so far, hadn't lessened her interest in sex. Sex with Luke, that was.

CHAPTER TEN

OVER A DELICIOUS dinner, Luke and Kelsey talked about everything from postmodernism and pizza toppings to the hockey season. They didn't discuss her pregnancy or their plans.

The limo was waiting outside for them. Kelsey slid into the seat and rested her head on Luke's shoulder. "One of the symptoms is that I'm tired all the time," she muttered, and let her eyes drift shut.

When she opened them, the limo was parked on a wide expanse of tarmac beside Luke's sleek jetliner, the lights on its wingtips flashing red and green. She sat up straight. "I thought we were going to your place."

"We are. My place in Tuscany."

"I can't—"

"I'll have you back in lots of time for the first day of classes. You said you'd always wanted to go to Tuscany."

"If I'd said Borneo, would you have had a place there too?"

"I'd have found one. We'll do our planning on the terrace under the olive trees instead of in your apartment, and a bed's already made up for you on the jet."

"You're taking over my life again."

"Smart as well as beautiful—you're quite the woman."

Kelsey scowled at him. She could make a scene on the

tarmac in front of the chauffeur and the pilot, or she could get on the plane and fly to Tuscany.

Kelsey got out of the car and marched toward the sleek silver jet.

She slept her way across the black waves of the Atlantic and the dawn light over France. Luke, fortunately, was up front with the pilot when she locked herself in the luxuriously appointed bathroom for a bout of morning sickness. As they descended into the small airport north of Florence, she applied a generous coat of make-up to hide the after-effects. The landing was so smooth as to be barely perceptible; they passed through Customs, then Luke led her outside to where his car was parked. The air was warm; the car was a scarlet Maserati.

Noticing her looking at it, he said, a touch defensively, "I love this car."

Briefly Kelsey forgot her predicament. Running her fingers over the cream leather upholstery, she said with a smile, "I can see why."

"I bought it two years ago. I've had it opened all the way on a couple of racetracks—never on the highway."

He flipped the trunk and put their bags in. "It's a two-hour drive to the villa, in eastern Tuscany. The nearest town's Cortona. You'll like it there, I promise."

That word again, he thought. What was it about Kelsey that made him keep saying it? "We'll loop around Florence, cross the Arno and head south-east. We could drive into Arezzo one day, see Piero della Francesco's frescoes."

"I'd like that," Kelsey said. But first, she thought, they had to talk. Serious stuff. Her little apartment was scarcely big enough for her alone. What would happen when she added a baby? If Luke were to offer her an allowance while she was at school, so she could find a bigger place, would she accept it for the baby's sake?

It was fine to have a spine stiff with Yankee pride. But pride didn't buy diapers or a stroller or a crib.

Maybe Luke was right: they *did* have to plan their strategy together.

Because she was fretting over all this, she only woke to the scenery when they were in the country. "New leaves on the trees," she marveled. "People have windowboxes out already—you didn't tell me it would be spring here. Oh, look, is that an olive grove? The leaves are all silvery. And look at the town on top of the hill, the lovely red roofs."

Cortona loomed over the plain, its medieval towers golden in the sun. Then the road branched through forests of sweet chestnut, beech and oak, light dancing through the fresh green leaves. The driveway to his villa wound past iron gates through a formal Renaissance garden. The villa itself, of the same vintage, was built of faded pink brick, with simple arched windows in perfect proportion to the whole. An elegantly colonnaded loggia overlooked a courtyard, where a fountain of dolphins splashed exuberantly.

"We're a little too early for the roses," Luke remarked. "I'll bring you back in May, when poppies and oxeye daisies are flowering in the fields. Or August, when the sunflowers are out—van Gogh would have loved them."

"I'll be in class in May," Kelsey said tersely.

"Your classes end Friday morning and don't resume until Monday noon," he said with a bland smile. "Lots of time for a quick trip over here… Let's go inside. Carlotta will have breakfast ready on the terrace."

So a few minutes later Kelsey was basking in the sun on the tiled terrace, where grapevines clambered over the wall and more rose bushes were coming into leaf. She ate ricotta with honey, and *panforte,* a dark cake flavored with cinnamon and cloves, accompanied by ripe strawberries, baked custard and freshly squeezed orange juice.

"Luke, you're spoiling me rotten." She gave him a quick smile, raising her glass in a toast. "You even remembered milk."

"Gotta watch out for the kid," he said flippantly.

His coffee cup stalled in midair. The kid. His kid. A girl with chestnut curls like Kelsey's? Or a boy with his own blue eyes?

"What's wrong?"

Luke came back to the present, to Kelsey's fingers fastened around his wrist. He shoved the images back where they belonged, dropped his head and kissed her palm. The little pulse at the base of her thumb began to race; his own speeded up to match it.

He said abruptly, with none of the finesse that he'd planned, "We'll get married on the weekend. My London CEO has a friend who's a clergyman, he'll fly over. And I'll make sure your brothers get here, too. We'll have a short honeymoon here at the villa, then you can move into my place in Manhattan and go to art school from there."

White-faced with shock, Kelsey sagged in her seat. "Hold it," she gasped. "Did you say *married?*"

"Don't look so surprised. Marriage is the only logical course of action."

"Logical?" she repeated blankly. "What's logic got to do with it? People get married because they love each other, not because it's a *logical course of action.*"

"Maybe if a little more logic was applied, the divorce rate would go down," he said dryly. "We're getting married because you're pregnant."

"*We're* pregnant."

"Okay, okay." *We. Our kid.* He couldn't get his head around it. In a voice of steel, he said, "No child of mine's going to grow up without a father and a mother living in the same house. Without stability and continuity. That's non-negotiable."

"Sounds to me like the whole thing's non-negotiable!"

"Much as I'd like to, we can't put the clock back," he said

curtly. "I'm more responsible for this mess than you are, because I was the one with experience. So I'm looking after the results."

Her temper rose another notch. "Mess," she said flatly. "Results. Funny thing, I thought we were talking about a baby."

"We are. Dammit, that's why we're having this discussion."

"Which you hate as much as I do."

"From the start I told you marriage wasn't for me."

"In time you'll hate me, then. Resent me. What good will it do for our child to grow up in a household where the father doesn't want to be married to the mother? Get real, Luke. Single-parenting's very far from the worst option."

"No," he said.

Her voice rose. "And that's what you call discussion?"

"We're going to do this right."

"Perhaps you're forgetting something. Marriage wasn't in my plans either. The baby's a fact of life. The timing's atrocious, and we're both responsible for that, but I need as much freedom as I can get because I've done without it for years. Marry you? That's not freedom."

"Single parenting sure as hell isn't freedom."

"I'll manage," she said stubbornly.

If he'd ever in his wildest fantasies imagined asking someone to marry him, he'd pictured her accepting instantly, ecstatically happy to be his chosen bride. Welcome to the real world, Luke thought. Kelsey looked ready to chew him up and spit him out.

"Let's begin again," he said, trying to rein in his anger. "Fact number one, we're great in bed. Fact number two, I respect you. Respect's fundamental, Kelsey, it's the basis for any half-decent marriage."

"How about fact number three? You don't love me and I don't love you. How can we bring up a child together when we don't love each other? *Love* is what's fundamental, Luke."

"So you've bought into all the romantic rubbish we're fed on radio and TV?"

She sat up straight, the sunlight gleaming in her hair. "Don't insult me. I grew up with two parents who loved each other, deeply and enduringly."

"Then you were exceptionally lucky," he said brusquely.

"What happens if we do get married, and then one or the other of us falls in love with someone else? Are we going to get divorced?"

"I won't fall in love." His smile didn't reach his eyes. "It is not on my list. But neither is divorce. We're marrying for the long haul—because marriage is a promise. It has to be."

That word again, she thought. "It certainly was for my parents. They used to argue passionately. Then we'd catch them in a clinch against the refrigerator door—pretty embarrassing for a kid. But all four of us knew they loved each other. We counted on it. Luke, we can't bring up a child on logic and respect!"

"Yes, we can. Logic, respect and stability."

"Stability," she said slowly. "That's the second time you've mentioned it. Just how long did you live with your mother?"

"That's none of your business."

"I'm probably not going to marry you anyway—but unless you tell me why you've got a phobia against commitment, and why you run like a jackrabbit whenever I talk about your mother, I sure as heck won't."

Luke pushed back his chair, metal scraping against tile. Standing up, towering over her, he said, "Oh yes, you will."

Surging to her feet, Kelsey glared up at him, her brown eyes blazing. "Is your mother still alive? Do you ever see her?"

"Did your brothers ever steal anything?" he retorted. "Rifle through the Dumpster outside the fried chicken outlet because they were hungry?"

"No," she whispered, her fingers gripping the edge of the table. "Is that what you had to do?"

Furious with his own outburst, Luke grated, "My mother died years ago. And you'll marry me, Kelsey. I don't give a damn if marriage is the last thing either of us wants, or if we both lose our freedom. Our child is going to have two live-in parents. You and me."

Kelsey gazed at him in silence. Her head was filled with a single image, that of a little dark-haired boy who'd been hungry enough to steal garbage from a dumpster. What freedom had he had? And how fortunate her own life had been in comparison.

Her sandals almost soundless on the tiles, she walked around the table and put her hand on Luke's sleeve. But with a gesture whose savagery shocked her, he struck her away. "Don't feel sorry for me."

She replied fiercely, "I feel sorry for the little boy you were, the one who had to paw through scraps to find something to eat. I'd have to have a heart of stone not to feel sorry for him."

Her words cut Luke to the quick. How the hell was he going to step back from confidences he'd never meant to share? More to the point, what was it about Kelsey that made him break rule after rule?

Going on instinct, he pulled her toward him. Her softness, her warmth, made the length of his body shudder. Taking her chin in one hand, he plundered her mouth, and felt her lace her tongue with his as she pressed herself against him.

Somewhere deep in the woods behind the villa a bird sang four clear notes. Luke swept Kelsey up into his arms, briefly burying his face in her hair. Then he marched across the terrace and carried her indoors, along the vaulted hallway with its inlaid marble floor, gilt chandeliers and potted palms. His gaze trained straight ahead, he climbed the polished sweep of the stairwell.

Kelsey wrapped her fingers into the folds of Luke's shirt, hanging on tight. Her chest was roiling with emotion, uppermost of which was, strangely, hope. Making love with Luke would, she knew, give her the intimacy with him, the emotional connection, that she craved and that they both needed. How else to heal the wounds of the past?

Luke strode down another wide hallway where two vast oak wardrobes flanked a flourishing fig tree. Pushing open his bedroom door with his foot, he pulled it shut behind him. His bed was a four-poster, covered in rich velvet. Antique rugs lay on the floor, sheer curtains hazing the light that fell across the bed.

"It's been so long—too long," he said harshly, and lowered her feet to the floor.

"Yes," she said, knowing exactly what she was going to do.

Enveloped in the burning blue of his eyes, she undid the zipper on her dress, pushed it from her shoulders and let it fall to the floor. Her stockings were thigh-length; she slid them down her legs, along with her lace-edged panties, then unclasped her bra, tossing it to the floor as well. Sitting on the edge of the bed, she swung her legs up and lay back on the glowing red velvet.

For a moment Luke stood still as a statue. Her skin was the cream of ivory, her hair a chestnut tumble, her eyes like woodland pools. His heart juddering in his chest, he stripped off his own clothing. He'd die if he didn't have her, he thought, and heard the words echo in his head, knowing them to be true.

It was too late to walk away. Much too late.

And it was nothing to do with pregnancy.

Like someone who'd hungered for something all his life, he fell on her, his mouth finding hers, his hands frantically relearning every curve and hollow of her body. And he was aware through every nerve he possessed of how she met him more than halfway, her body all fluidity and grace, so beautiful it made his heart ache in his chest.

Hunger ignited hunger. Need sparked need. Female to his

male, his mate...suckling, devouring, destroying and destroyed, Luke gave himself over to her keeping.

Their limbs entangled, sweat slick on his torso, they rose to their knees. He clasped her by the buttocks, suffused with the perfume of her skin, its flavor and delicious smoothness; their kiss was so deep he could scarcely breathe. Abandoning any attempt at control, he threw her back on the pillows and entered her in one swift stroke.

She gasped his name, her face convulsed. Burying himself, feeling her inner throbbing like his own, he hurtled toward the edge and felt her rise to meet him, her body a taut arrow of longing. Shattered, they fell together.

His breath harsh in his throat, Luke collapsed beside her. Raw, irresistible need, he thought blankly: he who'd planned ever since he was eight never to need another human being.

He closed his eyes, feeling naked in a way that had nothing to do with his body. Be damned if he was going to need Kelsey. Now or ever. That was one rule he couldn't afford to break.

Once again she'd made him lose control.

She stirred in his arms, saying softly, "Luke? That was wonderful...long overdue."

His face was hidden in the curve of her shoulder. He made a noncommittal noise, wishing he'd never met her, wishing he was anywhere but where he was: in bed with a woman who drove him out of his mind. Yeah, he thought. Out of his much-vaunted mind, all his cleverly constructed rationality lying in shreds around him. "You okay?" he muttered.

She nodded, lying still. Their bodies were still joined, the weight of his arm heavy on her ribs. His breathing stirred her hair. Why, then, did she feel suddenly, horribly lonely?

So suddenly aware of danger?

Luke had made love to her without once calling her by name, this man who was insisting on marrying her.

Earlier, in three brief sentences, he'd given her a glimpse

of a boyhood she couldn't begin to imagine. As her heartbeat slowed to normal, she was haunted by images of that little boy scavenging for food, begging on the streets. Where had his mother been? Why hadn't she looked after him?

Luke was marrying her so he could be a father to their child. Give the stability and protectiveness to their son or daughter that he himself had never received.

How could she deny him that opportunity?

She was trapped. She had to marry him.

CHAPTER ELEVEN

KELSEY'S THREE BROTHERS flew in the following morning, so it was early evening before Kelsey and Luke found themselves alone. She was wearing a dress of finely pleated cotton, her hair drawn back with two combs; she looked fragile and on edge. She said, "Did my brothers put you through it today?"

"Yes," Luke said, "and I think the more of them for it. They love you. Of course they're going to check me out."

You screw her around, man, we'll take you apart had been Dwayne's parting shot, but Kelsey didn't need to know that.

"I suppose you're right." She took a deep breath, wrapping her arms around her chest. "Luke, there's something I have to say. If you're having doubts—second thoughts about this wedding—it's not too late to call it off." She gave a wintry smile. "Brothers or no brothers."

His jaw tensed. "We're not calling it off."

"I want you to be very sure of what you're doing. These promises we're going to make tomorrow, they're huge."

He'd been doing his best not to think about them. "We have to, though. For the child's sake."

Pain lanced through her. "It's *our* child. Not some anonymous baby."

Luke strode over to the nearest window, pulling the drapes

over a star-spattered sky and the smallest of crescent moons. "I'll call it what I want."

"We're rushing into this too fast. We should wait a while."

"For what? You'll only get more pregnant, not less."

He might have intended it as a joke, but his voice was as cutting as a knifeblade. "I'm changing your whole life!" Kelsey cried. "Don't think I'm blind to that."

Luke didn't bother denying it. "That first night I took you to bed, I'm the one who walked into your room. If I'd left you alone, none of this would have happened."

She bit her lip, trying to stop it trembling. "I can't bear to be married to someone who feels forced into it. Against his wishes."

"Nice sentiments, Kelsey—but they're too late in the day."

His eyes were like chips of ice. She said bitterly, "I was brought up to accept the consequences of my actions. But I never thought I'd have to go this far—trapped in a loveless marriage. Luke, won't you reconsider? You could give me a small monthly allowance instead. You'd never miss the money, but it would make all the difference in the world to me."

"No," he said.

"You're not even hearing me out! You'd always have access to our child, I'd never refuse you that. But please don't force me into a marriage neither of us wants."

"I'm not going to be a father every other weekend," Luke said violently. "I'm in this full-time and for the duration. It's not that complicated. I don't see why you don't get it."

"You'll live to regret this marriage," she said with painful truth. "Both of us will. All three of us."

Hardening his heart against the strain in her face, he rapped, "Just make sure you show up tomorrow—don't take off at the last minute."

"Where would I go? Hide behind the altar in the village church? Skulk in the vineyard? I'll show up. What choice do I have?"

Had either of them had a choice since the moment he'd seen her at the top of the stairs in her skintight orange shirt? Luke said, "I had a selection of wedding dresses flown in from Rome. Carlotta put them in your room. One o'clock tomorrow. On the patio." He glanced at his gold watch. "It's time we joined the others for dinner."

Kelsey felt more like throwing plates at the wall rather than eating from them. Chin held high, she walked out of the room ahead of her prospective husband.

THE NEXT AFTERNOON, under a simple awning on the terrace, Glen, Kirk and Rico were standing with Luke and the gowned clergyman waiting for Dwayne and Kelsey to appear. A dove was cooing in the trees. The sun fell warm on the stones.

Luke's throat was dry and his shoulders tense. His mother had broken every promise she'd ever made him. But Kelsey, who had said she'd marry him, wouldn't break her word. Would she?

How well did he really know her? Right now she might be bundling her clothes into her suitcase, ordering the village's rattletrap taxi, heading for the airport... Luke rubbed his palms down the sides of his trousers and from the corner of his eye saw movement. He turned his head.

Kelsey, her hand resting on Dwayne's sleeve, was walking toward him over the stone tiles. She had chosen a simple white gown, full length, her arms bare. Her veil was net, falling to her shoulders. Her bouquet, which he'd also had flown in from Rome, was a sheaf of white lilac; they reminded him of the lilac bushes that grew around her old house in Hadley.

Her grace, her composure, stabbed him to the heart. She'd kept her promise. Of course she had.

He should never have doubted her.

Staring straight ahead, she took her place at his side. The clergyman began to speak, investing the words with all their ancient power. Dwayne gave her away, Glen took her bouquet, and Kirk lifted her veil. Her beauty, so well known to Luke, caused his voice to falter as he spoke the first vow.

However, rather than paying attention to the promises he was making, he found himself wondering just why she was marrying him. Sure, he'd been forceful in the extreme. But Kelsey, who'd climbed up a Virginia creeper because she'd been worried about him, and who'd raised the three stalwart young men who were now flanking him, was perfectly capable of saying *I don't* rather than *I do*.

When he'd first told her they'd get married she'd refused to even consider it. What had made her change her mind?

He'd forgotten to ask that all-important question. He was losing his grip.

Kelsey, however, didn't say *I don't*. She made her own responses clearly, still avoiding Luke's eyes; he slipped the antique gold ring he'd found in the little jewelry shop in the village on her finger. If she was feeling any emotion, he thought, she wasn't sharing it with him.

The benediction was pronounced, he kissed her briefly on the lips, and stepped back. Carlotta and her husband Mario signed the registry as witnesses, then bustled off to get the champagne and platters of food that were waiting in the kitchen.

Kelsey had met Carlotta, and had added to her small store of knowledge about Luke the fact that both Carlotta and Mario were extraordinarily loyal to him. Glancing up at her new husband, whose raven-dark hair was shot through with Tuscan sunlight, she said, "You'd better eat plenty. Carlotta stayed up most of the night cooking."

He'd done it, Luke thought. He'd married the woman who was standing at his side, who was carrying his child, and whose skin had the bloom of ripe peaches. She was smiling at him very naturally; it was an act, of course, but one he had to admire.

Now all he had to do was decide how he was going to handle a marriage that had come out of left field.

"Carlotta likes you," he said. "She told me it was about time I found myself a real woman."

"And I'm not even Italian."

Kelsey turned away to embrace each of her brothers, and then Rico, who kissed her warmly on both cheeks. She treated herself to one small glass of champagne, feasting on crostini, *panzanella* and *arrosto misto*. Afterward, Luke and she accompanied the clergyman, her brothers and Rico to the airport, then drove back to the villa.

Now that she was finally alone with Luke, Kelsey could think of nothing to say. One word was pounding in her head like a primitive drumbeat. Married. Married. Married.

She should have run away while she had the chance.

Carlotta and Mario were waiting on the terrace to toast the newlyweds. Mario's remarks made Carlotta blush and Luke laugh. He responded in Italian, Carlotta blushed some more, and finally Luke and Kelsey were left to themselves. As they strolled across the patio toward the villa, Kelsey said, "What was that all about?"

"The width of your hips and my virility."

"Oh." With a huge effort, she pasted a smile on her lips. "Virility, huh? Gonna prove it to me?"

Luke said casually, recognizing it for a moment of decision, "It's late, Kelsey, and you must be tired. Why don't you go to bed and I'll be along later?"

Her lashes flickered. "I'm not that tired."

"If you're eating for two, you should also be resting for two."

"I'd never do anything to harm the baby," she said evenly.

"Good." They'd reached the door to her bedroom. He leaned forward and kissed the tip of her nose. "Sleep well. I'll see you in the morning."

Turning on his heel, Luke walked away, and his thoughts walked with him. Something deeper than logic had driven him to marry Kelsey, he knew that. He knew, too, that he'd thereby broken one of the major rules of his life. No wife. No wife, no children, no intimacy, no needing—ever again—another person. Everything under control, just the way he liked it. Oh, yes, she'd changed his whole life, he was under no illusions about that.

So now he was going to take charge. He couldn't do anything about the wedding or the child. But there was plenty he could do about the rest. He was going to begin this marriage as he meant it to continue: with himself in the driver's seat. If sex with Kelsey churned up emotions he didn't want to deal with, making him need her in a way he deplored, then that was easily fixed.

He could live without sex.

He didn't need Kelsey. He didn't need anyone.

THE HONEYMOON WAS over.

Not that the honeymoon had ever really begun. Kelsey lay in bed—her own bed, in her own bedroom—in Luke's luxurious penthouse and listened to the small sounds of her husband getting dressed across the hall. He'd scarcely touched her since their wedding day; late last night, when they'd arrived here, he'd shown her to her room, which was entirely separate from his, then disappeared to check his emails.

Great sex been one of the reasons he'd married her, or so he'd said. So why was he shunning her? And what was she going to do about it?

Right now, nothing. She couldn't get out of bed, because as soon as she got vertical she'd be dashing to the bathroom for her usual bout of morning sickness. "Luke?" she called. "What time will you be home?"

He walked into her room, adjusting his silk tie. "Six-thirty at the latest," he said. "We'll eat out. I hired a cook; he'll start the same day your classes begin. Six days a week."

She said coolly, "You hired a cook?"

"His name's Marcel. Highly recommended. You won't have time to cook dinner once you're going to school."

Her classes started in three days. "It won't take him all day to make dinner."

Luke frowned into the mirror, adjusting the knot on his tie. "He'll do the groceries, get you breakfast, that sort of thing. Later on we'll throw a post-wedding party. I have an events coordinator who'll look after it. I have to go, Kelsey, I've got a nine-thirty meeting."

He gave her a brief peck on the cheek. "See you tonight." Moments later, she heard him leave the penthouse. She swung her feet to the floor, stood up and scurried to the bathroom.

At least she got this over with first thing, she thought a few minutes later, as she rinsed out her mouth, scrubbed her teeth and dashed cold water over her face. Taking her time, she looked around the bathroom. Black polished marble, etched glass doors, black-framed mirrors, a white tiled floor. The towels were black and white, too.

Did she want to wake up every morning to stark black and white? It might be fashionable and trendy, but it was about as welcoming as a hearse.

Why had Luke hired Marcel the cook without consulting her first? She'd have no privacy.

Was she crazy? Someone to cook dinner for her—hadn't that been her fantasy for the last ten years?

And this party Luke had mentioned sounded like a done deal. No consultation. No *What do you think, Kelsey? Should we throw a party?*

She pulled on her robe, her movements jerky. Maybe she should tour her new home instead of standing around complaining: a home nearly as new to Luke as to her, as he'd only moved in four months ago.

All the rooms were beautifully proportioned, with tall windows, polished parquet flooring, elegant ceiling moldings and a minimal amount of furniture. Minimal, too, was anything of a personal nature; certainly there were no photos of Luke's mother. The overall effect was about as cosy as a barn.

A decent barn would be cosier.

The rooms echoed to the sound of her footsteps. The view of Central Park, leafless under the winter sky, assaulted her with a desolate wave of homesickness.

This was her home now, Kelsey thought stoutly. All she had to do was make it into one.

How could it become a home if he refused to sleep with her? And why did that matter so much? She wanted her freedom; she should be delighted he was leaving her strictly alone. But already she missed the incredible intimacy of making love with him, the joy she found in his arms when their bodies were entwined.

She'd ask him pointblank what was going on. She wasn't going to take this lying down. Which was, she thought wryly, a very bad pun.

In the meantime, she was going shopping.

WHEN HE LET himself into the penthouse at twenty past six, Luke could smell food. He tested the air with his nostrils. Curried beef. Hadn't he told Kelsey they'd eat out?

Then she walked into the hallway, holding out a glass of wine. She was wearing a simple dark green dress, her hair in its usual tumble over her shoulders, her cheeks flushed.

She looked very beautiful; calling on all his will-power, Luke armored himself against her. He took a big gulp of the wine. Complex and richly layered, it slid over his tongue; if he wasn't mistaken, it was a bottle of Château d'Ampuis he'd been saving for a special occasion. "You picked a good one."

"I can't tell one label from another—I closed my eyes and pulled a bottle out of the rack. Dinner's nearly ready."

"I made a reservation at Cisco's."

"You can cancel it." She stepped closer. "I really wanted us to have our first meal at home tonight."

"Home?" he repeated inscrutably. He'd never had a home. Never wanted one. "This is just a place I hang my hat."

"Two hats now," she said flippantly.

He had no idea what was going on; it wasn't a sensation he cared for. "You cooked dinner?"

"Me and the deli four blocks away."

"Going all domesticated on me, Kelsey?"

Her lashes flickered. "Do you have a problem with that?"

Suddenly impatient, he plunked his wine glass on the tooled leather surface of the nearest table. "Are we having our first married fight?"

"Nope. It's a preliminary skirmish."

In spite of himself, his lips twitched. "I can see I've got a lot to learn."

She looked up, her eyes enormous. "We both do, Luke. I guess that's one of the things marriage does—speeds up the process."

Marriage, he thought. My wife. Kelsey is my wife.

He hadn't yet used those words to her or anyone else. Even mentally he had a tendency to trip over them. He said roughly, "Can you turn the dinner down? I've had a helluva day and I need a shower."

"Sure can."

As she disappeared into the kitchen, Luke took another sip of wine, savoring it on his tongue. A woman waiting for him after work. Dinner on the stove. *I'm changing your whole life…* That was what she'd said. He should have paid more attention.

With an impatient sigh he marched into his bedroom and loosened his tie. By the time he'd tossed it and his shirt on the chair, Kelsey had joined him. Her cheeks by now bright pink, she said, "Why don't I have a shower with you?"

Begin as you mean to continue. He said casually, "Better

not… I'm starving, didn't take time for lunch. I won't be a minute." Then he walked into the bathroom. But Kelsey followed him, watching his face in the mirror.

"Well," said Luke. Ruby-red towels hung on the rails; on the long counter was a huge bunch of silk flowers, the same glowing shade. A deep-piled ruby-colored mat lay on the tiles.

She said rapidly, "This didn't cost you anything, because I've got lots of money now I don't have to pay for the apartment. Do you like what I did, Luke?"

Money, he thought. We haven't talked about money. "The whole room's come alive," he said slowly.

She flushed with pleasure. "So you don't mind?"

"No…I like it." Was this what she meant about making a home? Maybe it wouldn't be so bad, after all.

Her smile was laced with relief. "There's more," she said. "In the dining room. But first things first." Turning around, she lifted the heavy mass of her hair. "Undo my zipper for me, would you?"

"Kelsey," he said flatly, "this isn't the time or the place. Off you go—you wouldn't want dinner to burn."

Her head jerked around. "Are you always in a bad mood when you come home from work?"

"I don't want to be propositioned the minute I walk in the door, if that's what you mean."

Stabbed to the heart, she said, "You don't have a worry in the world—it won't happen again." Then she marched out of the room, closing the door sharply behind her.

Two choices, she thought, arms crossed tightly over her breast. Lock herself in her bedroom and weep, or serve dinner as if nothing had happened.

Did she really want Luke to know how easily he could hurt her?

Weeping was out. She walked into the kitchen and gave the curry a vicious stir.

* * *

AS THE DOOR closed behind Kelsey, Luke stripped off his clothes.

Control, he thought. Himself in the driver's seat. Fine words. But he should have realized how hellish difficult it would be to turn his back—literally—on the woman who was now his legally wedded wife.

If he didn't want intimacy, he couldn't have sex. Not with Kelsey.

But he didn't want it with anyone else.

With an impatient sigh, he turned on the jets of water. A few minutes later, dressed in jeans and a cashmere sweater, he made his way to the kitchen.

Her voice perfectly even, Kelsey said, "Will you help me serve the dinner?"

Taking spoons from the drawer, Luke started dishing up the rice and a medley of root vegetables. This was not his usual scene. Domesticated, that was what it was. A word he'd always avoided like the plague.

He marched into the dining room with the loaded plates, then stopped short. There were sapphire-blue placemats on the table, and a vase of fresh irises, blue-purple with gold hearts. Kelsey said, "I couldn't resist the flowers."

"I've never bought you flowers," he said, a strange ache in his heart.

"You bought my lovely bouquet," she said, with something approaching a smile. As his gaze flew to the walls, she added, "They're four of my favorite paintings. I hope you don't mind—the walls were so empty."

More vibrant colors, these infused with the playful energy that was so characteristic of Kelsey. "I'd been planning to buy something for those walls…but I'd rather have your work hanging there."

"I saw the most wonderful carpet today. Antique Persian," she said. "It would look fabulous in here. I'll watch for the sales and come up with something just as nice, though."

"Which brings us to the subject of money." Luke tucked in to the curry. "Give me the bills for what you spent and I'll reimburse you."

"No, you won't! I didn't even check with you before I spent all that money."

"Let's get something straight from the start," he said levelly. "I'm the one with the money; you're a struggling art student. Therefore I pay the bills."

"I'd be using you," she said in an unfriendly voice. "I won't do that."

"For once, you can swallow your Puritan conscience. I'll get you a credit card tomorrow and set you up with your own bank account—then go buy the carpet."

"You haven't even asked what it costs!"

"We've gone past preliminary skirmish here—and it's a fight I'm going to win."

"I can't live off you. I won't."

Any number of women had wanted to do just that. "You married me for richer as well as for poorer," he drawled. "Rich is what I am. Very rich."

"How rich?" she said suspiciously.

As he named an amount, her eyes widened in disbelief. "However did you make that much money?"

"Years ago I discovered a talent for playing the stock market. Started small and it was uphill all the way. I'm a lot more diversified now—I can afford to be." He raised his glass to her. "So you can buy fifty carpets, plus a bar of red soap for the bathroom."

"We're in this together," Kelsey said with a stubborn tilt of her chin. "I have to make a contribution, or else I'm just a cipher. A kept woman."

"I'd never describe you as a cipher," Luke said tersely.

"And you're not a kept woman, dammit—you're my wife." There, he'd said it, and his very expensive ceiling hadn't fallen down.

"If I'm your wife," she said, in a voice from which she carefully ironed any emotion, "why won't you sleep with me?"

"That's my business," Luke said, and knew it was a weak reply.

"Our business, I'd have thought."

"Marriage wasn't in my plans, Kelsey—I'll handle it the way I see fit."

"That's sure on a par with the way you forced me into it. No discussion, no negotiation."

"It's how I operate. I didn't get to the top by being Mr Nice Guy."

"I'm not a stock certificate or a holding company—I'm a flesh and blood woman!"

Didn't he know it? He said coldly, "In the meantime, I pay the bills and you buy whatever you like—when I come home from work tomorrow I want to see the Persian carpet on the floor."

Kelsey let out her breath in a sharp sigh. "Aren't you worried that me and your credit card might go berserk?" she retorted. "Buy up the whole store?"

"Go ahead," he said. "Let me tell you something, Kelsey. You're the first woman I've ever met—apart from Sister Elfreda—who hasn't wanted to dip her hands into my money as deep as they'll go."

"That's the whole point—it's *your* money."

"We used the old-fashioned marriage ceremony, remember? I endowed you with my worldly goods. End of argument."

"It doesn't mean I have to use them, and you're not fighting fair."

"I didn't promise to fight fair. Nor did you. You only have to weep, Kelsey."

"Oh." She widened her eyes artistically, allowing them to swim with tears. "Like that?"

"Yeah," he said, "like that."

She said smugly, "I did amateur theatrics in Hadley. I was their champion weeper."

"Drink your milk," he said. "Living with you isn't going to be boring."

"Same's true of you." She got up, her gaze openly challenging as she bent to kiss him with all the sensuality he'd taught her. "Guess what? You're going to limit the cook to afternoons only, five days a week. He can prepare dinner and leave. That way, if I decide to seduce you on the new dining room carpet, I won't have to worry about some guy in the kitchen chopping celery."

The heat of her lips had burned through Luke's defenses; it took every ounce of his control not to reach out for her. "So that's why you want a carpet," he said.

She gave him an innocent smile. "Why else?"

Had he really expected her to meekly accept his refusal to go to bed with her? "Now you're the one who's not fighting fair," he said grimly.

She raised one brow. "This isn't only about preserving the spontaneity of our sex life, Luke—there are other things in life besides you. I need privacy in the mornings, whether it's to scramble my own eggs or paint a masterpiece."

Direct hit, he thought wryly. "I'll speak to Marcel tomorrow."

"Well, that was easy… I made a fruit salad for dessert. Watching my calories," she finished gloomily.

She was far too clever and too experienced a fighter to push him about the sex, Luke thought; anyone who'd raised three young boys to manhood would have learned a thing or two about strategy. He said mildly, "I hired Marcel to give you as much freedom as possible."

"That was nice of you," she said, with a suspiciously sweet smile, and raised her glass of milk in a toast. "To us, Luke."

"To us," he echoed, and wondered what the next step would be in her campaign.

CHAPTER TWELVE

ON THE FIRST day of her classes, Luke had an early meeting downtown; Kelsey thought he'd already left when she made her usual rush to the bathroom. Crouched on the floor, shaken with convulsions, she suddenly heard him call, "Kelsey, you okay?"

"Yes," she croaked, and wished him a million miles away.

"What's up?" The door pushed open.

"Go away!" she wailed, just before she was seized with another bout of sickness.

Then he was beside her on the floor, his hands gripping her shoulders, a note in his voice she hadn't heard before. "Morning sickness—why didn't you tell me?"

"It's done," she muttered. The heat of his fingers through her robe seared her flesh; to feel him so close, his breathing wafting her throat, filled her with a longing so deep it edged on pain. She wanted to lean against him, drawing strength and comfort from him; she wanted, she thought with a little jolt of her nerves, to be held by him forever.

But what could be less romantic, less conducive to passion, than morning sickness? She mumbled, "I need to wash my face."

Luke lifted her to her feet, watching as she cleaned up. She was as white as the sink, he noticed, her eyes blue-shadowed. "You do this every morning?"

"I'm lucky. One dose and it's over. It shouldn't last much

longer—I bought a book about pregnancy, and that's what it says."

"Are you sure you're all right?" Luke said. "I should go, I'm meeting a visiting Japanese market analyst. But why don't we delay the party until you're feeling better?"

Kelsey reached up to kiss him on the cheek, and was achingly aware how his body tensed against her. "We don't need to do that, I'm anxious to meet your friends. See you at six-thirty? I asked Marcel to make corned beef hash for supper; it's Glen's favorite."

Corned beef hash would make an interesting combination with the antique Persian carpet, Luke thought, picking up his coat from a chair in the living room. A book was lying on the coffee table. The book about pregnancy that Kelsey had mentioned. He picked it up too, then let himself out the door and ran down the stairs. If the book took his mind off the vulnerable curve of Kelsey's nape, the slender bones of her shoulders, it would have served its purpose.

The limo was waiting for him. Although his chauffeur was an excellent driver, no one could avoid the traffic jams of early-morning Manhattan. Opening the book at random, Luke started to read the chapter on miscarriages. While the authors stressed that sexual relations weren't harmful during the early months, Luke rather doubted they had in mind the heated, tumultuous passion that could flare between him and Kelsey at the slightest touch.

Inadvertently, by shunning her since the wedding, he'd been protecting her and the baby.

Wasn't that the man's role?

How was he supposed to know? No one had protected his mother from her own mother's wrath, or from the dangers of poverty on the streets. Nor had anyone protected him as a little boy. Least of all his unknown father. Yet he, Luke, would become a father before the end of the year, and be expected to know what to do.

His mind made another all-too-obvious leap. This baby wasn't going to stay a baby; it would grow up. Boy or girl, it would take away its mother's freedom for years. A freedom Kelsey had scarcely had the time to enjoy before she'd tumbled into bed with him. He remembered her list, written in red ink, recalled her fierce opposition to marrying him and felt a physical pang of what was surely guilt.

An emotion new to him.

In one night of passion he'd stolen something from her, something irretrievably precious that she'd more than earned.

Better for her if she'd never met him. Underneath it all, was that what she thought, too?

But the more he stayed away from her, the more freedom she'd have. That was straightforward enough. Basically, he'd been following the right course of action ever since the wedding; he just hadn't thought all his motives through.

Griffin Tower appeared just two blocks down the street. His priorities for the next four hours were to stop thinking about Kelsey and to pick the brains of the market analyst.

The latter he could handle. No problem.

He didn't need Kelsey. He wasn't going to allow himself to need her. Which might just be the biggest challenge he'd set himself in his entire life.

As soon as Luke had left, Kelsey went to have her shower. The hot water gradually eased the tension in her muscles; afterward, wrapped in a ruby-red towel, she found herself wandering into his bedroom.

Sunlight was slanting through the open drapes to lie in brilliant panels on the floor, the pillow was still indented where he'd slept, the sheets crumpled. Obeying a compulsion stronger than reason, she lay down on the bed, pressing her cheek to the pillow, the elusive scent of his body teasing her nostrils, haunting her with all that she lacked.

She wasn't so naïve as to think that if she and Luke made love all would be well between them. But she'd have the passionate certainty that she was desirable and wanted, and the intimacy so essential to her well-being. She'd never in her life felt as close to another human being as when she was lying in bed with Luke, his naked body pressed to hers, their thighs entwined. In his arms, hadn't she felt encompassed, ravished...loved, even?

She knew that was ridiculous. She didn't love Luke any more than he loved her.

The words she used didn't really matter. What mattered was that ever since their wedding she'd felt isolated, lonely and completely out of her depth.

She needed a strategy. Several strategies, she thought unhappily. Had there ever been a man as close-guarded as Luke?

The grandfather clock in the hallway chimed the half-hour. With an exclamation of distress, Kelsey got to her feet, grabbing at the towel. She had to get ready for class; she didn't want to be late on her very first day.

If Luke would only take her in his arms and kiss her as if she mattered to him, she wouldn't ask for anything more.

KELSEY FELT EXTREMELY nervous by the time she got home the following evening. Ridiculous, she thought. No reason to be scared. Her purchase was a very logical one, if rather belated, and certainly one on which she'd spent her own money, not Luke's.

She was late, because the detour had taken longer than she'd expected. She'd wait until after they'd eaten; candlelight and one of Marcel's delicious dinners would ease the way. For wasn't she hoping her gift would break the stalemate between her and Luke, that somehow it would bring him close to her once again, releasing his passion and the passionate intimacy she longed for?

She was fighting for her life, she thought as she hung up

her coat. How melodramatic that sounded; nevertheless, it rang true. Her gift was, so far, the only strategy she'd been able to conjure up.

Luke came out of the living room. "How did your drawing class go?" he said, kissing her lightly on the cheek.

"Is that the best you can do?" she said pertly.

His blue eyes hooded, he took a sip from his wine glass. "Did you have a live model? Or was it a still life?"

"Still life," she said, lowering her lashes to hide a hurt she should be used to by now. "The class went well, and I'm reading some fascinating stuff about perspective for an essay we've been assigned."

Luke followed her into the kitchen. "Smells good," he said. "Spaghetti Bolognese and Caesar salad."

As she lifted the lid on the saucepan, her wrist looked impossibly delicate; her cheekbones were shadowed. "You look tired," Luke said slowly.

"I am—these first days of classes are like a whirlwind. But I'm learning so much."

"Want me to light the candles?" he said, and escaped to the dining room. His tactic was simple enough: keep Kelsey at arm's length. Unfortunately, it didn't seem to get any easier. For a dizzying moment he could almost taste the little pulse at her wrist, her lips' soft curves, the taut buds of her nipples; cursing himself under his breath, he went back to the kitchen to bring in the plates.

He was stirring cream into his coffee when Kelsey said in a rush, "I bought something today."

As he glanced up, she added, "Something major."

His nerves tightened. "Another carpet?" he said lightly. "I'm sure I'll like it. I've liked everything you've bought so far."

"It isn't for the house, it's for you. I—just a minute, I'll get it."

Although he had no idea what to expect, wasn't that one

of Kelsey's charms? She came back in, carrying a small jeweler's box, and thrust it at him with none of her usual grace. "Here."

He knew the jeweler's name, a dealer in antique rather than contemporary pieces. Curious, Luke opened the box. A gold ring rested on black velvet, its design two clasped hands, a man's and a woman's.

"When we got married, you gave me a ring," Kelsey gabbled. "I didn't have the chance to buy you one in Tuscany. I saw this ring in the window yesterday and fell in love with it. So they cleaned it for me, and I picked it up on the way home today."

Her words echoed in her own ears. Fell in love with it? With a ring? Luke was staring at it, making no move to take it out of the box.

"Don't you like it?" she whispered.

"Why did you marry me, Kelsey?" he said quietly. "I know I was pretty damn forceful…but you still could have said no."

Her heart gave a nasty little lurch. "At first I *did* say no, remember? I was scared of marrying you. Really scared. Moving to the city, finding out I was pregnant, the meeting we had in your office after not seeing each other for so long…it was overwhelming."

"What made you change your mind?"

Frightened, because the conversation wasn't going the way she'd anticipated, she said with a gaucheness rare to her, "I had to marry you, Luke. Our baby deserves a father, and you deserve the opportunity to be a father—you never had one of your own."

Because Kelsey had integrity she'd had no choice. That was what she was saying, Luke thought heavily. She'd put his needs—and the baby's—ahead of her own, just as she'd put her three brothers' needs ahead of hers years ago. But this time he, Luke, was responsible for caging her in. "I see," he said.

"Luke, if you don't want the ring I can take it back. Lots of men don't wear them—I should have checked with you first."

"No," he said, "I don't want you to take it back." He knew her well enough to realize the ring was important to her. The fact that it would remind him, day and night, of how he'd robbed her of so much potential was his problem. "Why don't you put it on for me?"

For a moment Kelsey looked at him in silence. Unreadable, inscrutable Luke, she thought in sudden, crippling despair. "I don't have a clue what you're thinking— are you sure you want it?"

He did his best to produce a genuine smile. "Yes. I like the design, the two hands—it's very cleverly done."

Clumsily she took the ring out of the box. While she'd waited at the jeweler's she'd envisaged Luke smiling into her eyes as she slipped the ring on, then taking her in his arms, holding her, kissing her, perhaps even carrying her off to bed.

Opening to her in the way she craved.

Right now he looked like he'd rather be on the first plane out of there.

Fumbling, she managed to push the ring onto his finger. "There," she said. Gathering all her courage, she brought his hand to her lips, then lowered it to rest against the soft swell of her breast.

A muscle twitched in Luke's jaw. He tugged his hand free. "You don't give up, do you?"

"You scarcely touch me anymore!"

It was a cry from the heart; the passionate emotion in her voice only hardened Luke's resolve. Giving Kelsey as much freedom as possible and protecting the baby were real enough reasons to keep his distance. But he knew, deep down, that he was really protecting himself. "This marriage is going to be on my terms," he said.

She said bitterly, "I wonder how you'd treat me if you didn't respect me."

"Kelsey, I don't want to keep on fighting about this. Go

have a hot shower, change into something comfortable and put your feet up."

"Get out of your sight, in other words." Pride stiffening her spine, she pushed back her chair.

In the bathroom, she found herself staring at the ruby-red towels as if she'd never seen a towel before. Luke hated the ring. Did it remind him, forcibly, of his predicament—married to a woman not his type, who was pregnant with his child?

It would never have been his choice to marry her.

Or become a father.

Ironically, her gift of a wedding ring had shown her how deeply Luke resented their hasty marriage.

Shivering with something deeper than cold, Kelsey pulled off her clothes, bundled her hair under a cap and stepped into the shower. She hadn't felt so alone, so frightened and off-balance, since the day she'd discovered she was pregnant. Even her heart felt cold—cold enough to shatter into a thousand pieces.

She lifted her face to the jet of hot water, trying to relax. Water ran down the black and white marble, streaking it like tears. She should have stuck with black and white: ruby-red spoke of a myth, romantic and deluded.

You look tired, he'd said. Was that a euphemism for unattractive, boring and dull? Or was it another way of saying that, pregnant, she no longer aroused him to passion? She glanced down at her wet body. Her waistline was disappearing, her belly had a pronounced curve. Blue veins traced her breasts.

It was women like Clarisse who attracted Luke: model-thin, elegant, and definitely not pregnant. No wonder he'd been keeping his distance since the wedding. She no longer turned him on.

Kelsey discovered she was crying, her tears joining the water already streaming down her cheeks. She swiped at her face. She'd had more than a week to get used to her loveless marriage, and she'd known from the very first day she'd met Luke how aloof and unapproachable he could be. So why did she care so much?

Anyone would think she was in love with him.

Her mouth dropped open. Choking on the spray, she backed off, gazing at the black and white marble. She *was* in love with him. Why else did her heart leap in her chest when she heard his key in the lock, or her body melt when he brushed her cheek with his lips? Why else was she standing here weeping?

For a moment Kelsey closed her eyes, letting the feelings well up from deep within her, banishing her sadness. She loved Luke, heart and soul.

She wanted to burst into song. She wanted to run barefoot through a meadow of wildflowers, splash through the waves on a tropical beach.

She wanted to throw her arms around him and tell him.

But she couldn't. Luke didn't love her; telling him would add one more weight to the burden he was already carrying of an unwanted wife and an unplanned-for child. No, she couldn't possibly tell him.

It was her secret, to be borne as best she could.

She felt cold to the bone again. Quickly Kelsey turned off the jets and dried herself, dressing in stretchy black pants and a loose sweater. She had to get herself under control, stop this seesawing of her emotions before she faced Luke again.

She had an enormous amount to be thankful for, she thought fiercely. His money, no question, had eased her life immeasurably. She was taking lessons from teachers she already revered, who would deepen and intensify her work. And last, but by no means least, her health was good and her pregnancy, according to her doctor, was proceeding just as it should.

Trying to hold these thoughts, Kelsey went to her bedroom,

propped herself up on the pillows and began to read, taking notes as she went. Two hours later, Luke walked in the room.

"Past your bedtime," he said. "I'm going to the video store to pick up a movie."

He was the same Luke; yet, because she loved him, he was unutterably different. The impenetrable depths of his eyes, the strength of his jaw, his taut, rangy body: it was as if she was seeing them for the very first time. She dropped her eyes. "I'll finish the book tomorrow," she said, pulling her nightgown from under her pillow.

The drapes were drawn against a cold rain; the lamplight cast a circle of warmth and intimacy. Luke's pulses quickened, his blood thickening in his veins. He reached for the hem of her sweater.

Kelsey's heart gave a great leap. To make love with Luke, knowing she loved him…that was what she needed. Scarcely breathing, she waited.

His hand dropped to his sides. "I may go to the office while I'm out," he said in a clipped voice. "Don't wait up…I'll see you in the morning."

Then he was gone. Kelsey got undressed, folding her clothes with exaggerated care, and got into bed. Raindrops beat against the panes. Wind whined around the corner of the building. Sleep had never felt so elusive.

She had no idea how long she lay open-eyed in the darkness, or whether she'd drifted into a restless sleep. But suddenly she was wide awake, sitting up in bed with her heart pounding in her ears. A floorboard creaked in the living room; someone was in the penthouse.

The digital clock told her Luke had only been gone for half an hour. So it wasn't him. Grabbing her robe, she slipped it over her shoulders and crept across the floor. The nearest phone was in Luke's room, across the hall.

Not stopping to think, because if she did she'd be cowering

in bed with the covers over her head, Kelsey opened her door with exquisite care. Soundlessly, she took four steps out into the hallway.

A book dropped with a small thud in the living room. Glued to the floor, she heard footsteps coming toward her, and closed her eyes in sheer terror.

"Kelsey—what's wrong?"

Her eyes flew open. The floor dipped and swayed. Luke grabbed her before she could fall, pulling her against him. "Are you ill? Is it the baby?"

Her breath was locked tight in her lungs. Clinging to him, she stammered, "I thought you were a b-burglar."

"A burglar?" He gave a humorless laugh. "My thieving days are long gone."

"You said you were going to the office...so I didn't think it could be you."

"I changed my mind." Luke lifted her chin in his fingers, his irises ablaze with emotions she couldn't begin to guess. "If you thought I was a burglar, what the hell were you doing wandering around the place in your nightgown?"

Braced by his anger, she retorted, "What was I supposed to do? Wait to be murdered in my bed? I don't have a phone, Luke. The nearest one's in your bedroom, and I don't sleep there, remember?"

His muttered curse made her blink. "Dammit, I never thought of that. Kelsey, I'm sorry. I decided against the office because it was raining so hard."

Briefly he rested his face in the hollow of her shoulder, his breathing warming her bare skin. She buried her hands in his thick hair, massaging his scalp with a little purr of contentment. Her whole body sprang to life, desire and love miraculously entangled.

Then Luke raised his head. At the V of his shirt his pulse was hammering, but his blue eyes were shuttered against her.

"Will you be able to sleep now? I got a movie, and I'll close the door in the den so I don't disturb you."

But I want to be disturbed... The words hovered on the tip of her tongue. She'd always been a fighter, and wasn't she fighting for far more than herself here? But somehow the brand-new knowledge that she loved him paralyzed her. Feeling absurdly self-conscious, she faltered, "Come to bed with me and hold me, Luke—just until I fall asleep."

He winced inwardly. How could he refuse? He'd have to be made of stone not to see how badly he'd frightened her. Taking her by the hand, he led her back into her bedroom. As she pulled back the covers, he lay down on the bed, fully clothed.

She slipped into his arms, burying her face in his shirtfront. "I feel safe with you here," she whispered.

Luke lay still, listening to the rain slapping against the windows, steeling himself to think about anything other than Kelsey's softness and warmth, so intimately pressed to his body. Scarcely breathing, praying she'd fall asleep, he watched the red numbers click by, one by one, on the digital clock.

Eventually her breathing slowed and deepened, and her arms loosened their hold around his waist.

He didn't want to leave.

Moving very carefully, Luke got out of bed and left Kelsey alone in the big bed.

CHAPTER THIRTEEN

TWO DAYS BEFORE THE PARTY, Kelsey had decided she needed a new dress. She might be pregnant, but that was no reason not to look her best. Recklessly she had gone back to the same store where she and Luke had shopped before they'd flown to the Bahamas. There she'd found a gown in a shimmering gold tissue that made her look radiant and blooming.

How deceptive appearances could be, she'd thought wryly, and had paid for the gown herself.

Now, one hour before they were due to leave, Luke came into her bedroom, where she was putting the finishing touches on her make-up. "Don't let me forget I've only got mascara on one eye," she muttered, trying not to notice how lethally attractive he looked in his tux.

Luke stared at her in the mirror like a man transfixed. Because she was leaning forward her cleavage was exposed, the creamy slopes of her breasts and the shadowed valley between them stabbing him with a vicious hunger. "Doesn't matter if I haven't seen you for five minutes, five hours or five days," he said thickly, "I never think you can possibly be as beautiful as you are."

Hope flared in Kelsey's breast. So he still found her beautiful... Turning, she kissed him on the mouth, letting all the love in her heart speak for her. His arms hardened around her, and for a moment she thought she'd won. Then, his fingers like steel bands, he pushed her away. "I have something for you," he said.

Keeping his hands steady with a huge effort, Luke took a box out of his pocket and opened it. A teardrop diamond pendant on a slender gold chain rested on black velvet, with matching earrings that dangled on tiny gold links. As he looped the pendant around her throat, it blazed against her skin.

In the tall mirror, Kelsey looked at herself in silence. Then she said quietly, "I've come a long way from Hadley."

For once, Luke couldn't read her. "You're the same woman—fancier clothes, that's all."

She made an indecipherable sound. "You didn't need to buy me any more jewelry."

"I wanted to."

So she wouldn't disgrace him in the company of his peers? She was scared witless about this damned party, Kelsey realized. It was one thing to get married in the company of Rico and her three brothers, another to face Luke's friends, business associates and, no doubt, former mistresses. Wishing with all her heart that he loved her, because then she could face a thousand strangers, Kelsey took the earrings from the box and fastened them at her lobes.

"Thank you, Luke." She looked stunning, she thought dispassionately, and carefully brushed mascara to the lashes of her other eye.

She couldn't cry; she'd smear her make-up.

An hour later she was in the thick of the party. In one way it wasn't as bad as she'd expected, mostly because Luke stayed close to her side, introducing her and fielding the conversations so that she was always included. But in another way it was worse, for as the music struck up he took her in his arms and whirled her onto the dance floor. Automatically she followed his lead, her gaze trained on the gold studs in his collar. So near and yet so far, she thought, feeling a wave of the despair she'd grown to dread wash over her.

She couldn't show her feelings; she had far too much pride for that. She said lightly, "I feel like Cinderella."

"Just don't vanish at midnight," Luke said, a flick of grimness crossing his face.

She gave him a dazzling smile. "Where would I go? I've burned my bridges, Luke. You know that as well as I do."

"I'm not convinced a burned bridge or two would stop you," he said.

So he wasn't as sure of her as he seemed, Kelsey thought. But then, he had no idea she'd fallen in love with him.

Her secret, and hers alone.

As the song came to an end, she clapped politely. The ballroom was decorated in gold and white, with a profusion of elegant scented lilies; chandeliers glittered in crystal splendor from the molded ceiling. The buffet, with its ice carvings and exquisite array of dishes, made her think of her brothers; they'd make a clean sweep of it.

She danced with Luke's personal secretary, with a Belgian diplomat and then a Greek shipping magnate, and said all the appropriate things, smiling until her face ached. As the guests congregated around the buffet she ate sparingly, chatting with a Scandinavian CEO and his cool blond wife, and staying away from the wine. Then, squeezing Luke gently on the sleeve, she said, "I'm going to freshen up— back in a minute."

He smiled at her as though she was the only woman in the room. Not for her benefit, she thought with an inner quiver of fury, but for the benefit of all his friends and associates. He said easily, "I'll stay around here so you can find me again."

On her way to the restroom she was snared by three groups of people, but finally she made it. There were yellow and cream freesias on the marble counter, she noticed, and locked herself in a stall. Briefly she leaned her head against the louvered door. It was good to be alone.

How she loathed pretending that she and Luke were a pair of devoted newlyweds. Nothing could be further from the truth.

A group of women came in, chattering loudly. When one of them said, "I adore your dress, Clarisse," Kelsey froze in position.

"Valentino…I picked it up in Paris last week. Well, darlings, what do you think of the new bride?"

"She's very pretty."

"Luke's certainly sticking close."

Clarisse gave a malicious laugh. "For now. Luke never sticks close to one woman longer than six months. We all know that."

"Luke never *marries* his women—we all know that, too," another woman said snidely.

"She trapped him—got herself pregnant, darling. Oldest trick in the book. Once the brat's born, you won't see Luke for dust."

"Clever of her, you've got to admit. Imagine the alimony."

"A little nobody from nowhere," Clarisse sneered. "Going to art school—have you ever heard anything so ridiculous?"

"Stop fretting, Clarisse. He'll be back in circulation before the year's up. We all know that. What do you think of Dior's new perfume?"

Feeling physically ill, Kelsey leaned on the door. A few moments later, the women trooped out and she was alone again. How stupid she'd been not to realize that gossip must be rampant about Luke Griffin and his new bride, that the people who'd been so polite to her all evening were tearing her to shreds behind her back. And wasn't the gossip basically true?

She *was* pregnant. He *was* trapped.

For better, for worse, she thought wearily. For Luke wouldn't divorce her; not, at least, while their child was young enough to be affected by a separation. How long would that be—eighteen years? Twenty?

It felt like a life sentence.

In the gilt-edged mirror Kelsey reapplied her lipstick and practised smiling. When she was satisfied that none of her distress showed, she pushed the door open. Luke was still standing by the buffet table, and the woman at his side was the woman whose photograph she'd seen in the society pages. Clarisse. In her Valentino gown.

So was she, Kelsey, going to scurry back to the wash-room and hide?

No way. This was her party. Hers and Luke's. Her place was at his side.

Kelsey wound her way through the crowd, smiling at new acquaintances, stopping to chat with a few, her head held high, pride in every inch of her bearing. Adrenaline was coursing through her veins by the time she reached Luke. He smiled down at her as she rested her left hand lightly on his sleeve. "Kelsey, this is Clarisse Andover. Clarisse, I'd like you to meet my wife, Kelsey."

Clarisse nodded coolly. "A party like this must be rather overwhelming for you."

"Not at all." Kelsey gave Luke a brilliant smile. "My husband wants to show me off—hard to find fault with that."

"Scarcely your usual scene. Given your background."

"I brought up my three younger brothers, Clarisse—a crash course in being adaptable."

"You'll need to be. Some of us, perhaps, know Luke better than you."

Luke's arm tensed under her hand. Smoothly, before he could say anything, Kelsey remarked, "Living with a man day and night, sharing his home and his bed, does away with the pretences of dating." She favored Luke with another intimate smile. "It's a lovely way to get to know someone."

She was lying through her teeth. But only Luke knew that, and he wouldn't tell.

Clarisse's voice thinned. "You're surely not so naïve as to believe in marriages that last?"

"I believe when a good man makes me a promise he'll keep it. In other words, I trust my husband."

"How sweet," Clarisse said with a vicious smile.

"How real, I would have said." With a strange pang of pity, Kelsey added, "I hope you'll move on and find happiness with someone else, Clarisse. The way we accept change says a lot about us, wouldn't you agree?"

"Wait a while—knowing Luke, you'll get more change than you like."

"I might not have known him as long as you," Kelsey said steadfastly, "but I'd be willing to bet my brand-new diamonds I know him better than you. By the way, I love your dress… Valentino, am I right?"

Clarisse's breath hissed between her teeth. Swiftly masking the fury in her violet eyes, she reached up to kiss Luke on the mouth; at the last minute he turned his head so her lips landed on his cheek instead. "I hope you'll be very happy, darling," she said to him, in the kind of voice that indicated she didn't think it likely. "I'll talk to you later."

As she stalked away, Kelsey said thoughtfully, "So that's Clarisse… I don't think much of your taste, Luke."

"She's a sore loser—the night you left the Bahamas she threw herself at me. When I told her to get lost, she ripped my character and my sexual prowess to shreds. So tonight she was doing as much collateral damage as she could." Luke gave a reluctant laugh. "You more than fixed her clock, Kelsey."

"I doubt it. She doesn't think her clock needs fixing." Kelsey batted her lashes at him, shoving to the back of her mind the ugly little scene in the washroom. "I want some of that delicious-looking cake and then I want to dance with you to work it off."

Luke said abruptly, "I didn't invite Clarisse, she came with someone else. But I should have given more thought to this damn party—dumping you in the midst of all these people, most of them strangers."

"I can hold my own," Kelsey said.

"Yes, you can." He looked right at her, and the crowds died away. "You told her you trust me…is that true?"

"Yes," she said, "it is."

He raised her hand to his lips, and kissed her fingers with lingering pleasure. "Thanks," he said huskily. "Cake, you said?"

The contact surged through her, filling her with a happiness that shone from her eyes. Luke wasn't telling her he loved her. But she'd touched him in one of those places he kept closely guarded; and that, for now, was intimacy enough.

THE DAYS PASSED. While Kelsey might have felt a momentary closeness to Luke at the party, the effect hadn't spilled over into their daily life. They were like two strangers, she sometimes thought, who'd been forced to share living space and who were stepping around each other with careful politeness. But they weren't strangers. Always hovering in the back of her mind was the closeness they'd once shared, the lovemaking and the laughter.

Had Luke been anyone else, she might have suspected he was having an affair. But she couldn't believe that of him: he might not want her anymore, but he'd keep the promises he'd made her, no matter what they cost him. She'd told Clarisse the truth. She did indeed trust him.

He was away a lot on business, leaving her to her own devices. Two weeks after the party he flew to Stockholm and Oslo for board meetings.

The day before he was due home, when several of the students were heading to the local bar after an unexpectedly tough exam, Kelsey decided to join them. The alternative was an empty penthouse, luxurious and lonely.

There'd been no bar scene in Hadley. She found she was enjoying the raucous music, amused by the sexual undertones as some of her companions flirted and danced, so she stayed later than she'd planned. She took a cab home, rode the elevator to the top floor, and inserted her key in the lock.

The door was hauled open. "Where the *hell* have you been?"

"Luke!" she cried, startled. "You weren't supposed to get home until tomorrow."

"I finished early." His fingers dug into her sleeves. "I was about ready to call the police."

"The police? What for?"

"I had no idea where you were."

All Kelsey's unhappiness coalesced into anger. "I'm twenty-eight years old, perfectly capable of looking after myself. And I'm not accountable to you for every minute of my time."

"When I get home to an empty place and no note, no message to say where—"

"You didn't let me know you were coming home early!"

"I wanted to surprise you," he said nastily. "Guess I did. Who were you with, Kelsey?"

His blue eyes were afire with emotions she couldn't possibly have named. But wasn't that better than the politeness, the distance she'd been living with for far too long? "Are you accusing me of being with another man?" she said incredulously.

"Just answer the question."

"After class a bunch of us went to a bar called Tony's— the local hangout for the artsy crowd. I ate a spinach salad, drank ginger ale and declined to dance. But I enjoyed myself, Luke—which is more than I've been doing with *you* lately."

Freedom, he thought. Tonight she'd been exercising her freedom. If he was smart, he'd give her a pat on the shoulder and keep his mouth shut. "Bored with me already?" he snarled.

"Tired of being treated like a stick of furniture."

"Don't be ridiculous—you're my wife."

"One more possession, that's what you mean. I'm also sick of being treated like bone china, as if I'll break if you look at me sideways."

"You're pregnant," he said shortly.

"It's not a disease. It's a very natural condition."

"I don't give a damn what you call it—you should have ordered the limo to come home."

"I took a cab. Be glad I didn't take the subway, or walk."

Luke wouldn't put it past her to do either one. Was that why he'd been gripped with such terror when he'd gotten home and found the penthouse empty? "For all I knew you could have been hit with a car. Or having a miscarriage."

She flinched. "If I have a miscarriage, you'll be the first one to know."

The words were out before he could censor them. "Then you'd have married me for nothing."

"So would you."

Into the silence, the phone rang. "That'll be Alex," she said, "wanting to know I got home safely."

Quickly she picked up the receiver. "Hi, Alex…yes, I'm fine, no problems getting back. Thanks a lot, and I'll see you tomorrow."

His fists bunched at his sides, Luke rasped, "Who's Alex?"

"Luke, we're not going down that road—he's an older student, with a wife and two kids, and he was being protective of me, that's all. Back off."

That another man should have to protect her only made Luke angrier. "From now on I want you to phone here and leave a message if you go out after class. That way at least I'll know where you are."

It wasn't an unreasonable request, but Kelsey didn't feel reasonable. "I often don't know where *you* are…you sure as heck aren't here much."

"You can always reach me on my cell phone," he said curtly. "I'll pick one up for you tomorrow—I should have done that weeks ago."

She didn't want to talk about cellphones. Temper coursing through her veins, Kelsey dropped her coat on the floor, kicked off her boots and forgot all about strategy. "I want to make love to you, Luke Griffin. Right now. On the floor, on the dining room carpet, or even in bed." In spite of herself, her voice broke. "How else am I to get close to you?"

"No," he said flatly, his fists clenched at his side.

Not for anything was she going to beg. Frantic to escape, knowing she was going to cry, Kelsey whirled. But she'd forgotten that she'd dumped her coat on the floor. As she tried not to trip on it, her socked foot skidded on the smooth parquet; with a yelp of alarm, she threw up her hands to save herself.

Luke flung himself forward and caught her, pulling her to his body. "You could have fallen," he muttered, feeling his heart stutter in his chest.

Kelsey burrowed her face into his shirtfront, inhaling his scent, so well remembered, so deliciously male. *I love you...* The words were on the tip of her tongue, aching to be released. As she looked up, wondering if she'd find the courage to say them, his head dipped, his lips sealing hers in a kiss so fierce, so full of desperate need, that she forgot everything else in the red heat of hunger.

Closing her eyes, she opened to him; his tongue invaded, sought, promised, filling her with a wild joy. Then he lifted her in his arms, burying his face in her tumbled hair. Could you die from happiness? she wondered, and latched her hands behind his head.

He had to have her, Luke thought. In his bed, naked and willing. He couldn't wait any longer, couldn't stop. For in one kiss hadn't she driven him beyond lust, beyond anything he could control?

Her curls were soft against his cheek, her breasts pressing into his chest. Stepping over the coat on the floor, he carried her into his bedroom. As he put her down, she reached behind her and pulled back the covers, then started tearing off her clothes, her gaze glued to his.

The open invitation in her eyes, the ripe curves of her body... In a fever of impatience, he flung his own clothes to the floor and took her in his arms, kissing her as though there was no tomorrow. Her tongue thrust to meet his; she rubbed against him, the fullness of her breasts tantalizing, arousing, ravaging him. Leaning down, he suckled her. She threw back her head, and with one sharp cry was lost.

"I want you," she gasped. "Oh, Luke, how I want you."

They fell together onto the sheets. Steeped in her scent, spinning out of control, Luke clasped her by the buttocks and entered her; she was more than ready, hot, wet, waiting. Again she cried out, and he felt from far away her inner throbbing as she rose and peaked and fell.

Consumed by her, his heart pounding in his ears like a primitive drum, Luke thrust, and thrust again. She wrapped her legs around him, so that he went deeper and deeper, until he couldn't breathe for wanting her. Panting, plunging, he felt himself crest. For a split second he held, then in an unstoppable surge emptied himself within her.

He dropped his head to her breast, panting harshly, struggling to bring himself back from a place he'd sworn he wouldn't go. Kelsey was holding him around the ribs, palms pressed to his spine, her heartbeat racing in his ear. "Oh, God, I needed that," she muttered.

So had he. Obviously. But he'd done exactly what he'd vowed not to do—allowed his passion free rein, taken Kelsey by storm.

Out of control. Drowning in intimacy.

He said, striving to sound casual, "I swear I won't do that every time you go to a bar."

"Too bad," she said lazily. "I was thinking I should go to Tony's every night."

"Too much ginger ale's bad for you." He lifted himself off her. "Go to sleep, Kelsey, you've had a long day."

Her lashes were already drifting to her cheek. "Sorry we had a fight," she mumbled. "But it was a wonderful way to make up." Within moments her breathing had steadied and deepened.

Luke got out of bed; he'd sleep in his own room. If he didn't, he knew damn well what would happen sometime through the night: he'd make love to her again, tap into that firestorm of emotion that she could so easily arouse in him simply by existing.

So much for willpower. So much for control.

CHAPTER FOURTEEN

FREEDOM AND DESPAIR, thought Kelsey. It was a weird combination.

She was standing by the living room window on an afternoon in May. Spring had arrived in Manhattan, the trees in Central Park a sprightly green, the sky a cheerful blue.

Normally she loved spring, with its aura of new beginnings.

But this year she was too unhappy to appreciate it. She was beginning to wonder if she'd dreamed that hasty, passionate lovemaking in Luke's bed; it was as though she'd had a taste of paradise, only to have it snatched from her.

After much soul-searching, she'd come to the unhappy conclusion that Luke had only made love to her out of sexual deprivation. Certainly he'd kept his distance ever since.

Her body suddenly tensed as she heard him come in the door. When he walked into the living room, she saw with a spurt of rage that he was carrying flowers. He said, holding them out to her, "Tulips. You must be missing your garden at this time of year."

A dutiful wife would smile and thank him. But the rage had gone from a spurt to a torrent, and Kelsey didn't feel either dutiful or grateful. "You can put them in the kitchen," she snapped. "I'll find a vase later on."

Luke looked at her in silence. Her cheeks were patched

with hectic color, and the light streaming through the window was coiled like copper fire in her hair. He'd wondered when this confrontation would happen, and was rather surprised she'd waited so long. Dropping the tulips on the counter, he said, "What's up?"

"Are you sure you want to know?"

"Let it all hang out, Kelsey."

"I've wasted my time and your money buying red towels and Persian carpets. I thought if I added some color to this place I could make a home out of it. But you're never here, so how can it be a home?"

"I'm here right now."

"In the last three weeks you've been away for thirteen days, at the office until nine p.m. four nights, and glued to the TV the rest of the time—you call that being home?"

"I've been staying away on purpose," he grated. "You're a smart woman. You must have figured that out."

"We haven't gone to a concert or a play for weeks. You're ashamed of me, aren't you? That's why you keep disappearing. You don't want to be seen with me in public because everyone knows I trapped you into marrying me."

"What the hell are you talking about?" he said blankly.

"At the party I overheard Clarisse and some of her friends saying how cleverly I'd played my cards, and how much alimony you'd have to fork out once you decided 'a wife and a brat'—I quote—weren't to your taste."

His breath hissed between his teeth. "Consider the source."

"I've made you the laughing stock of the financial world, Luke. The brilliant businessman duped by a woman from the sticks."

He stepped closer, gripping her by the shoulders. "That's garbage and you know it. I learned a long time ago that when you rise above the pack, the pack will do its best to bring you down. So I've cultivated a thick skin and gotten on with my life. It looks as though you may have to do the same, and for that I'm sorry."

"If you're not ashamed of me, then why haven't we been to the latest Broadway hit, or the new exhibition at the Met?"

"There hasn't been time."

His fingers were digging into her flesh; he was standing so close she could have reached up and traced the carved line of his mouth with her finger. Balling her fists at her sides, she seethed, "That's not a real answer."

"I've been giving you as much freedom as I can," he said irritably. "Time to spend with your fellow students. Time to study. Time to paint in your new studio."

She felt a pang of guilt. How could she be so angry with Luke when he'd spent a small fortune having the solarium in the penthouse remodeled into a studio for her?

To hell with guilt. "You've been to Bangkok, Paris, Stockholm and Oslo in the last couple of weeks. You've talked more on your cell phone than you talk to your wife. You call that giving me freedom? I call it avoidance."

His own temper rising, Luke said, "Remember the heading on your list? The one written in red ink back in Hadley? 'Freedom List,' it said. By getting you pregnant and insisting you marry me I've taken away that freedom. So I'm trying to compensate—give you as much space as I can."

"Maybe you should let *me* decide how much freedom I need."

"Deny I took it away from you."

"I did the same thing to you."

"So you don't deny it?" Smothering a pain much sharper than he cared for, he added, "I don't give a damn what Clarisse and her crew say, Kelsey. You'd never connive at trapping anyone into anything they didn't want to do."

"I used to bribe the boys with homemade chocolate chip cookies so they'd weed the garden and cut the grass."

"That's different. With them, you needed every advantage you could get."

Resting her palms on his chest, trying to subdue her anger, she gazed straight into his eyes. Summer-blue eyes, she thought, and gathered all her courage. "I don't turn you on any more, do I? Not like I used to. That's what the real problem is."

"You're kidding me."

"I wish. I'm into maternity clothes and I'm about as sexy as a hippopotamus."

"For God's sake, when you're nine months pregnant and you can't see your own toenails you'll still be the sexiest woman on the planet."

"Oh," Kelsey said, sudden tears flooding her eyes. "Really?"

"Don't cry. I can't stand it."

"If I'm that sexy, why don't we ever make love? You've been to bed with me once since we got married, Luke. Once."

He dropped his hands and moved away from her, staring out at the lacy mass of trees. "You think that's easy? It nearly kills me to stay away from you."

"Then why do you?"

"Partly to keep the baby safe. I totally lost control that one time. I can't risk that happening again—it's not safe for you or the baby."

"The pregnancy book said sex was fine."

"The kind of sex that happens when you and I get anywhere near a flat surface? I don't think so."

"So once we were married you decided we shouldn't make love," she said inimically.

"I figured we should cool it."

"You made a decision that affects both of us without consulting me, or letting me know you'd made it. You had no right to do that."

"It affects all three of us," he said. "And someone had to."

"I'd like to wrap those tulips around your neck!"

Luke said abruptly, "I've had enough of this. Let's go out to eat. Wear one of your new maternity outfits and I'll take you to Scranton's."

Her eyes brilliant, she walked right up to him and wrapped her arms, rather than the tulips, around his neck. Then she planted a kiss fueled by anger and desperate longing full on his mouth, rubbing her breasts against the hard wall of his chest.

He seized her hands and yanked them down to her sides. "Don't, Kelsey," he said in a raw voice. "Just don't."

She wasn't going to cry. She was not. "This isn't only about freedom and keeping the baby safe—there's more going on than that. You don't want intimacy, do you, Luke? You want to be in control, all the time, every minute of the day." She bit her lip. "When we're in bed together you lose control. And you hate me for it."

"Okay, so I don't want intimacy—what's the big deal?"

Going on intuition, she blazed, "When you were a little boy, why did you have to steal, and scavenge for food? Where was your mother when that was going on? Just what did she do to you?"

"That's none of your goddamn business!"

"If you don't want me walking out the door, you'd better make it my business."

Life without Kelsey…inconceivable.

Needles. He remembered them lying on the floor by his mother's bed. How he'd pricked his finger on one and how angry she'd been. He also remembered a drunken man forcing his way into the apartment, taking all the money from her purse and tossing a little bag of white powder on the table.

He'd been six years old.

As though a dam had burst, Luke let the words pour out. "The last time my mother left I was eight. We were living in a boarding house on the back streets of Boston. She'd been gone before, for three or four days at a time, and I'd learned to look out for myself. Drugs, Kelsey. She was hooked on drugs. So every time she'd had her fix, and the world was rosy, she'd promise things were going to change. She wouldn't let Bart's gang beat up on me any more. She'd take me out for fish and chips. She'd stay home nights."

"Beat up on you?" Kelsey faltered.

"I wouldn't join their gang. Didn't want to join any gangs. I was a loner even back then."

"And she didn't protect you?"

"Her promises lasted just as long as the fix. The last time she left I didn't get worried until four or five days went by. But it stretched into a week, and then Bart beat up on me again, so I had to steer clear of school. I was hungry, stole a bunch of bananas from a fruit stand. A cop was standing on the corner and saw me—so I ended up in the system. They found my mother in a back alley a couple of days later. Dead of an overdose."

"Oh, Luke…"

"Foster homes, running away, petty theft, juvenile court. I did it all. Then there was a blip in the system. I was sent to a convent for ten months, where I met Sister Elfreda." The deep furrows in his forehead smoothed; his reminiscent smile nearly broke Kelsey's heart. "She was a tough old bird, and she saved me from myself… I loved that woman."

"Is she dead, too?"

"Seven years ago. She's the one put me onto the orphanages. She didn't think much of my sex life, but she sure was happy those abandoned kids had a safe place to go."

Pierced to the core, Kelsey said, "I'm so glad she came into your life."

"If she hadn't, you and I wouldn't be standing here having this conversation."

Kelsey said flatly, "I'll never abandon our child…or make promises I have no intention of keeping."

He looked right at her, his eyes the vivid blue of a Tuscan sky. "I know you wouldn't."

"I'm so sorry you had to grow up that way." Helplessly she added, "*Sorry*...what kind of a word is that? No child should be exposed to the things you were."

Luke ran his fingers around his collar. "I never talk about my past. So why the hell am I telling you?"

"Because I had to know."

"After I inherited Griffin's Keep, found out about Sylvia and saw how she'd lived, I figured my mother had good reason to rebel. Who knows...? Maybe the drugs gave her something she'd always been denied. It didn't look to me like Sylvia knew much about love—tossing her only child out onto the streets for one lousy mistake."

"Now I'm the one who's pregnant," Kelsey said evenly.

"History repeating itself?" His jaw tensed. "Are you planning on walking out that door, Kelsey?"

"No," she said. "It's the last thing I want to do."

"Not even now, when you know the truth? Your husband's a thief who had a junkie for a mother."

"Did you steal or break the law to make your fortune?"

"Once I'd met up with Sister Elfreda? I wouldn't have dared."

She said, keeping her voice steady with an effort, "I'm so proud of you, Luke. You survived against terrible odds, you've made an amazing life for yourself, and you're doing your best to prevent other kids from walking the road you had to. Before we got married you said you respect me—how could I do anything but respect you?"

Luke stared at her; his brain felt paralyzed. Hadn't he always assumed that if he did tell any woman about his background she'd run as far and as fast as she could? But Kelsey was smiling at him, so beautiful that his heart ached in his chest. He said flatly, "You know more about me than anyone else in the world. Even Rico."

Tears pushed against her lids. "I'll take that as a compliment."
He'd had enough of talk. "Let's go eat."

"Luke, I'd so much rather we went to bed."

"Don't push me, Kelsey. Not right now."

"If you'd just hold me—we don't have to make love."

"No."

The finality in his voice was like a death knell. "All right,"
she said flatly, "let's go to Scranton's."

She might as well eat roast duck and *crème brulée* as sit
home and cry her eyes out. Much as Luke hated seeing her
cry, she knew a few tears wouldn't change his mind. Was there
anything she could say or do that *would?*

WHEN THEY GOT home from the restaurant, Kelsey went
straight to bed. Exhausted, she fell asleep right away. She
didn't hear Luke go to his own bedroom, much later. She was
dreaming, a mist-soaked dream in the dark of night…

She was walking along a beach. Waves reared from an
obsidian sea, lapping the sand with long white tongues. She
was alone. Or was she? Wasn't someone watching her from
the deep shadows between the trees?

She stopped in her tracks. Cold water sloshed around her
ankles, tugging at her as she gazed at the forest's impenetrable
wall. Something moved in the shadows. A face, she thought.
The face of the enemy. She hurried along the beach, desperate to leave the unknown watcher behind.

The sand was soft, her feet sinking deeper, deeper with
every step, until she could scarcely move. As a wave hit her
knees, making her stagger, a pallid moon penetrated the
clouds. Looking back over her shoulder, she saw the dark hulk
of a body emerge from the woods and start walking toward
her, slowly, as though there was all the time in the world…

A hand grasped her shoulder. "Kelsey, wake up! You're
having a dream, wake up."

With a yelp of sheer terror, she struck out, her eyes flying open. The man holding her was Luke.

Kelsey burst into tears, sobbing as though her heart would break. Luke gathered her into his arms, feeling her frame shudder as she wept. "You were having a nightmare," he said, "I heard you cry out."

She wrapped her arms around him as tightly as she could, his solidity and warmth like talismans against the night. "I was so frightened," she whimpered, fumbling to describe her unknown follower and the quicksand grip of the beach. "I couldn't escape, couldn't even move…"

Trapped, Luke thought grimly. That was what the dream had been telling her. He was the dark follower, from whom she couldn't escape; he was the one who'd mired her in quicksand.

She hadn't denied she felt trapped this afternoon when she'd confronted him. Rhythmically he began stroking her back, hearing her sobs subside as her body quietened in his arms.

She said raggedly, "Luke, I want you to do something for me."

"If I can, I will."

"Take me to Tuscany," she said. "Back to the villa."

"Why, Kelsey?"

Instead of answering, she burrowed her wet face into his bare chest. It was lust that stabbed him now, hot and imperative. Easing his hips away from her, he said, "We could go tomorrow afternoon, when your classes are done for the weekend."

"I know you just came back from Bangkok and you must be tired…but I really want to go. We have a three-day recess from school next week, so if you were free we could stay longer than the weekend."

How often did Kelsey ask for anything? "Sure, we can do that."

"I adored the villa," she said, her breath hitching in her throat, wafting his skin. "I felt I could be happy there. I—I just need to go back, that's all."

He already knew she wasn't happy here. Wasn't it to escape that knowledge that he kept flying around the globe on business he could very well have delegated?

Running away.

He'd never thought of himself as a coward. It wasn't a picture he cared for.

"The limo will pick you up after class, and I'll meet you at the airport," he said. "If you have time, pack your bag in the morning."

"I'll make time," she said. "Thank you, Luke."

It was an odd time to realize he didn't want gratitude from Kelsey. But what did he want in its place?

THE FLIGHT WAS unexpectedly turbulent, so Kelsey slept very little. It was pitch dark when they finally arrived at the villa. Carlotta had made a light supper, which Kelsey ate with her eyes almost shut. Then she tumbled into bed, knowing she couldn't possibly do The Big Speech tonight. It had kept this long. One more night wouldn't hurt.

When she woke up, she saw to her dismay that it was nearly noon, Tuscan time. She showered, dressed in an empire-waisted sundress with strappy flat-heeled sandals and her diamond pendant, and went looking for Luke. It was wonderfully warm outside, the roses blooming pink, cream and white against the faded stucco walls. Luke was sitting at the table, drinking his coffee, and in the few moments before he caught sight of her Kelsey feasted her eyes on him.

Raven-black hair, eyes blue as the sky, a body he'd refused to share with her, and a heart that was largely unknown to her. But that, she thought militantly, was going to change.

Then he glanced up and got to his feet, smiling at her with such unforced pleasure that she felt tears prick her eyes. "Carlotta's gone to the village because it's the annual parade later on," he said. "So she left breakfast here for you. Or is it lunch?"

"Brunch," Kelsey said. The sun glinted on his gold wedding band as he pulled out a chair for her. There was a big jug of roses on the table; inhaling their sweetness, she tried to loosen the tightness in her chest. It was now or never, she thought.

Never wasn't an option.

CHAPTER FIFTEEN

"I CAN HEAR the doves cooing, like they did on our wedding day," Kelsey said. She could also hear her pulse thrumming in her ears; she was about to use the very last weapon she possessed. "Luke, I came here to tell you something."

Luke's hand stilled as he passed her the brioche; a cold fist clutched his heart. She'd had time to think about his past and she wanted out. He said in a hard voice, "You're not leaving me—I won't let you."

"I told you—"

"Bringing me back here, where we got married, to tell me it's over? No way, Kelsey."

She grabbed a chunk of brioche, dismayed that he could so easily misinterpret her. "I don't want to leave you. But maybe you want to leave me."

"No," he said curtly, "I don't."

"Are you sure?"

"As sure as I'm sitting here smelling the roses. So, what do you want to tell me?"

Her cheeks as red as the roses, she announced, "I've fallen in love with you."

Luke stared at her, feeling as though he'd been hit on the head with a blunt instrument. Something akin to terror coiled to life in his belly. "You have this talent for taking me by surprise. Would you mind repeating that?"

"I'm in love with you."

"That's what I thought you said."

"I sure wasn't planning on falling in love. It just happened."

"You don't sound very happy about it."

"I'm not," she said, scowling at the tablecloth. "I've trapped you into a marriage you resent, I've taken away your freedom, and you don't love me. End of speech."

Trying desperately to marshal his thoughts, Luke said, "Let's be accurate about one thing. *I'm* the one who's taken away *your* freedom."

For the first time since she'd started talking, Kelsey looked full at him. "I want intimacy, Luke. Not freedom. How could I feel trapped when I love you and I'm bearing your child?"

He winced. "But you haven't been happy."

"You keep pushing me away." In spite of herself, her voice quivered; unconsciously, she was resting her hands on the gentle rise of her belly. "Until we had that big row a couple of nights ago I thought you couldn't stand the sight of me since I've started to show, that I was a complete turn-off. I know that's not true now. But nothing's changed."

Luke said harshly, "You'd more than earned your freedom—and then I got you pregnant. How do you think that makes me feel?" He answered his own question. "Guilty as sin, that's how."

She gave him a smile as wide as the sea. "I love being pregnant. Because I love you."

"I wish you'd stop saying that!"

"I wish you'd act more like a real husband."

"You scare the hell out of me, Kelsey. You stir up emotions I didn't know I possessed, needs so deep that all I can do is run. When I was a kid, I needed my mother. But she let me down. I can't afford to need you, don't you understand?"

With passionate intensity she said, "I won't let you down, I promise I won't."

"I'm so sorry I've hurt you."

His rough-spoken apology, one he hadn't known he was going to make, breached the last of Luke's defenses.

"I've been thinking a lot about my mother the last couple of days. Abandoned by the man who made her pregnant, kicked out of her home, left penniless with no skills. If I imagine you in that position I can hardly bear it."

"You'd never do that to me," Kelsey said softly.

He ran his fingers through his hair. "I doubt her own mother—Sylvia—ever loved her. How can I blame her for escaping from that pain with drugs? Or for not knowing how to mother me?"

"You forgive her. That's what you mean," Kelsey said, tears hanging on her lashes.

"Forgiveness?" he said blankly. "Is that what this is all about?"

"You had a terrible childhood, Luke. But there were reasons, there were extenuating circumstances. I saw Griffin's Keep. It wasn't the house of a woman who knew how to love."

His short laugh held no amusement. "You got that right. So you're saying I've forgiven my mother because now I understand why she behaved the way she did?"

"Our child won't be brought up that way."

He rubbed at the tension in his neck. "But there's a legacy, Kelsey. I'm not capable of loving anyone. I never learned how."

"You loved Sister Elfreda."

"That was different," he said shortly. "I'm talking about you. My wife. I doubt I can ever love you as you should be loved. It's not in me…and you deserve so much more than that."

Kelsey bit her lip, the conviction in his voice cutting

through her composure. What if he were right? "I've wanted so badly to tell you I'm in love with you," she said jaggedly. "It's taken me all this time to realize that love is a special kind of freedom. It makes me stronger as a woman. As an artist as well."

Luke looked at her in silence. The sun lay warm on her bare shoulders and lit the haunted pools of her eyes; as always, her beauty touched him in the place he'd always kept inviolate. She was so sure of herself, he thought in near despair. So wise. She made his defenses seem almost shabby. "Come to bed with me," he said hoarsely. "I want to hold you, make love to you. Maybe that's the best I can do."

She let out her breath in a small sigh. "I've missed you so much."

"I promise I'll give you whatever I can," Luke said, and knew he'd taken a major step toward commitment. Impulsively he plucked a rose from the jug, tucking it in her hair.

"Careful of the thorns," she murmured, smiling at him.

"I wouldn't hurt you for the world. Yet it seems that's all I'm capable of doing." He hesitated, adding with painful accuracy, "I'll keep right on hurting you if I can't give you what you want—it's inevitable."

She didn't want to believe him; she couldn't afford to. Kelsey lifted his hand to her cheek, holding it there. "Maybe I love you enough for both of us."

Somehow Luke didn't think it was that simple. His throat felt as though a stone was lodged halfway down; the terror in his gut hadn't gone away. Taking refuge in action, he swung Kelsey up in his arms and strode across the warm paving to his bedroom. The awnings were drawn against the noon sun. With all the tenderness at his command, he laid her on the bed and stretched out beside her. He began kissing her, slow, deep kisses, sinking into them, and all the while he was stroking her body, increasing the tension notch by notch.

At least he knew how to do this, he thought in a sudden flare of self-contempt. But love, a concept tossed around as casually as leaves tossed in the spring winds, was beyond him.

Was he going to be a hostage to the past for the rest of his life? Was that the best he could offer Kelsey?

Then she touched him, running her fingers the length of his torso so that an involuntary shudder of desire rippled through his muscles; the past dropped away. His eyes trained to hers, he stripped off his shirt.

Piece by piece they took off their clothes, until they were naked on the big bed. He trailed his lips down her neck to her breasts, to the tight shells of her nipples, hearing her moan his name; her body's curves were as fluid as the sea. Then, deliberately, feeling his heart thud in his chest, he laid his palm to the swell of her belly. He said, and knew the words for another promise, "Our child, Kelsey."

Her face was suddenly radiant. "Ours. Yours and mine. You'll be a good father. I know you will."

He wished he were as sure. "I'll do my best," he pledged through the tightness in his chest. Then, and only then, did Luke let his hand drift lower. Wishing only to give her pleasure, he played her until she was writhing under his touch, her eyes glazed with need. He tripped her over the edge, brought her trembling and ravaged to the peak again, and plunged into her, desperate for his own release.

"Now, Luke," she gasped. "Now…" And felt him throb deep within her, his face convulsed as they both fell into the storm's heart.

Kelsey lay still, limp and satiated. Joined, she thought. Enfolded. *I love you, I love you.*

What had he said? *I'm not capable of loving anyone.*

If Luke was never able to reciprocate what she felt for him, would she be able to bear it? She closed her eyes, blanking out a future she couldn't foresee.

* * *

AFTER A WHILE, Kelsey fell asleep in Luke's arms, her breathing slow and regular, her chestnut curls like tendrils of silk on the pillow.

He pulled away from her, knowing that for him sleep was an impossibility. Gathering up his clothes, he dressed, wrote her a quick note, and slipped out of their room. Outside, he set off up the slope to the vineyard; the trail was edged with chicory, white-faced daisies and scarlet poppies bobbing in the breeze.

Far from resenting their marriage and her pregnancy, Kelsey was wise enough to know that love augmented her, that he hadn't stolen her freedom. He believed her, and felt lighter for the belief; just as forgiving his mother had lightened a burden he'd scarcely known he was carrying.

He hadn't told Kelsey the whole truth when he'd said he'd loved only Sister Elfreda. As a little boy he'd also loved his mother. However, betrayal by betrayal, Rosemary had destroyed both love and trust; with all the passion of his eight years, he'd vowed never to love anyone again.

Sister Elfreda had prevented that vow from encasing him in ice. But as he'd grown to adulthood the ice had resurfaced; he hadn't allowed any of his mistresses close enough to crack it.

Until Kelsey came along.

Rosemary had broken promises right and left. Kelsey would never willingly betray him. He knew that as surely as he knew poppies were red.

The tenderness he felt when he held Kelsey in his arms; his passionate hunger for her body and his ever-deepening trust in her: could they be different aspects of love?

Perhaps love had as many brilliant facets as the diamond he'd given her.

Perhaps…was that the best he could do?

He entered the vineyard; the vines were espaliered to tidy rows of wire fences. Tight bunches of grapes were tucked, green and hard, among the leaves. The sun would ripen them and bring them to fruition, Luke thought, part of an age-old cycle.

She was his fate. His destiny.

Luke stopped dead in his tracks. He'd had to travel to the ancient hills of Tuscany to understand that.

But it wasn't enough.

Passing through the vineyard, he came to a grove of olive trees that rustled in the breeze, their trunks gnarled and limbs twisted. Sitting down in the shade, Luke gazed across the little valley to where his villa dozed in the sun. Kelsey was there, sleeping in his bed. His wife. The soon-to-be mother of his child. The woman who loved him with all the generosity of her heart.

For over an hour he sat still, watching the shadows edge their way across the brittle grass. It would destroy Kelsey to live with a man who didn't—couldn't—love her as she needed to be loved.

Leaning forward, he rested his forehead on his knees.

IT WAS THIRST that eventually brought Luke to his feet. His steps as heavy as his heart, he walked down the hillside toward the villa. The flowers in their careless profusion mocked him; he remembered the dream where Kelsey, lying in a field of wildflowers, had opened her arms to him, and that, too, mocked him.

He was a man regarded by many as a brilliant success. It had taken Kelsey to bring him face to face with himself, face to face with the scars of the past and the gaping hole at the center of his life.

He didn't know how to love; in a very real way, he was a failure.

Luke climbed the stone balustrade on the terrace and walked toward the villa, reluctance dogging his steps.

The bedroom was empty. Kelsey's sundress was gone, and on the back of the note he'd left she'd scrawled a few words.

Walking down to see the parade. Meet me by the bakery? I'm craving *panforte* and you. Love, Kelsey.

She'd drawn a little heart under her name and encircled it with roses.

Briefly he closed his eyes. Then he crumpled the note and shoved it in his pocket. He'd walk to the village. It'd be easier than taking the car, with the parade on. Leaving the room, he crossed the cool, tiled hallway.

His house keys were on the table. Just as he reached for them, Mario burst out of the kitchen, startling him. The old man was wringing his hands, babbling in Italian. "An accident, *signor,* a terrible accident."

Luke stood as if turned to stone. "Accident? Where? Who?"

"In the village, at the parade. A bull, Perlocchio's bull, got loose from the cart. It chased people, gored some of them… *Oh signor, signor.*"

Kelsey. She'd gone to the village to watch the parade. His blood froze in his veins. "Is Kelsey home? Is Carlotta?"

"Carlotta, *si, signor.* But the young mistress…"

"I'll go right now. Stay here in case I miss her and she comes home. Call me on my cell phone if you hear anything."

He raced outside, got in the Maserati and surged down the winding driveway, blind to the dappled shade of beech trees and the brilliant blue sky. Nothing had happened to her, to her or the baby. She was safe. She had to be.

He couldn't bear it if she wasn't. His life would be meaningless without her.

Meaningless. Empty. As cold and dark as the depths of the sea.

Love, the emotion he'd run from most of his life, now flooded him in a great wave, pulling him under, drowning him.

He loved Kelsey. Body, heart and soul, he loved her.

What if he'd left it too late to tell her?

Too late. The cruelest words in the language.

He'd loved her for weeks. For months. Ever since he'd seen her standing at the top of the stairs in her tight jeans, her hair a chestnut cloud around her face. He'd called it lust, which was true as far as it went. And then he'd run from her.

He'd cheated both of them in his refusal to see the truth. What a fool he'd been! An unutterable fool.

In a screech of brakes Luke pulled up at the outskirts of the village and parked outside the first of the little stucco houses. Slamming the car door, pocketing the keys, he ran over the cobblestones of the narrow street toward the tiny local clinic. Already he could hear the wail of an ambulance siren; fear sluiced his body.

The clinic was pandemonium. Three stretchers were lined up in the entrance, attended by two doctors in blood-spattered white coats. The stretchers were occupied by two elderly farmers and a little girl, her parents clutching her hands. Horrible, Luke thought, to feel simultaneous pity for the injured and relief that none of them was Kelsey.

He pushed his way down the crowded corridor, opening doors without compunction, peering inside, closing them swiftly. His heart was thudding in his chest; his hands were ice-cold. If he didn't find her here he'd search the streets, one by one.

He might, he supposed, find her at the bakery. Although it didn't seem likely.

A man's voice cried out in pain. A woman wailed her distress. And still no Kelsey.

The door was open on the last room down the corridor. He looked inside and saw her.

Her sundress was flecked with blood. She was standing by a gurney, her arm around a little boy. A young woman lay on the gurney, clutching the little boy's hand.

"*Va bene,*" Kelsey was saying helplessly. "*Va bene.*" And

all the while, in a language that was universal, she was stroking the boy's shoulder.

Luke stepped into the room and her head swung around. "Luke!" she cried out in relief. "Can you tell the boy that his mother's all right? She's not seriously hurt. A broken arm, I think, and maybe a dislocated collarbone. But I don't know how to tell him that."

"There's blood on your dress."

What was he talking about? Kelsey thought in confusion; he was as white as a ghost. She glanced down at her dress. "Oh...it must have happened when I helped someone earlier—I took first-aid courses when the boys were small."

He grabbed her by the arm, his fingers like steel bands. "So you're not hurt?"

"No. I'm fine. Please, tell the boy he doesn't have to worry."

Luke knelt to bring his eyes to the boy's level. In a quick flood of Italian he poured all the reassurance he could into word and tone, and saw the boy slowly relax.

"Grazie, signor," the mother whispered.

A doctor came through the door. Kelsey took the little boy onto her lap as the doctor examined his mother; more reassurances followed, then the mother was wheeled away for an X-ray, the boy clasping her good hand as if he'd never let go.

"Maybe we could drive them home once she has a cast on?" Kelsey said. "I think the father's away. Are Carlotta and Mario all right? I've been so worried about them."

"They're both home."

"It all happened so quickly; it was awful."

He put his arms around her. The heat of her body seeped through her dress, warming his hands. She was alive, she and the baby safe in his embrace. The nightmare was over.

In a great surge of gratitude Luke rested his cheek on her hair. She began describing how a balloon had burst, frightening the bull, which had broken its harness and rampaged down the narrow little street. "People were screaming, hiding in doorways, shouting for their children—it was terrible. But no one was killed. The men and the girl on the stretchers, they're going to be all right—one of the nurses spoke a little English, enough for me to understand." She gave him a tremulous smile. "Should we tell the mother we'll drive her home? We could send down a meal, too—Carlotta always makes enough for ten people."

"Carlotta had five strapping sons, and old habits die hard," Luke said, hearing his voice as though it came from another man. "Yes, we'll go find the mother. In just a minute."

He looked around the windowless room. Tongue depressors, scales, stethoscopes and the acrid smell of disinfectant: it was the least romantic of settings. Yet he couldn't wait until they were back on the sunny terrace, surrounded by roses. He tightened his embrace, feeling as though he never wanted to let her go. "I have something to tell you."

Her brow crinkled. "It won't keep?"

"No." He smiled at her. "I've finally come to my senses. Helluva way to do it, I know. I broke every speed limit in Italy after Mario told me there'd been an accident at the parade—God, Kelsey, I was so afraid something had happened to you."

His voice was unsteady; she noticed new lines carved at the corners of his mouth. "I was further up the street when the bull got loose. I'm sorry you were frightened for nothing, Luke. But shouldn't we go to X-ray now and—?"

"You're not paying attention."

"Maybe you should sit down," she said dubiously. "You don't look so hot."

"I aged ten years in the last half-hour. Hell, twenty years." He gave a cracked laugh. "Here I am, trying to tell you I love you, and you're not even listening."

She made a tiny, indecipherable sound, staring up at him

as though he'd lost his mind. "You're joking," she said. "This isn't the time or the place for—"

"See what I mean?" His voice deepened. "I'm in love with you, Kelsey. Head over heels in love with my beautiful wife."

"I got knocked out by the bull and I'm in a coma," she croaked. "Or else I'm fast asleep and dreaming."

Luke leaned down and kissed her parted lips with all his newfound love, their softness and warmth filling his body with something far beyond hunger. "Does that feel real?"

"Oh, yes," she said fervently, her heart giving a great swoop in her breast. "Tell me again, Luke. So I'll know I didn't dream it."

"I love you, Kelsey. I have ever since I went to your house and you told me you didn't want to have dinner with me. I was just too stupid—or too stubborn—to admit how much I needed you. To myself, let alone to you. I wanted everything under my control, including any emotion that looked like it was getting out of hand. But this afternoon, when I thought I might have lost you, that I'd left it too late—I never want to live through the last half-hour again."

With a shiver of dread, she pictured herself in his shoes. "Love leaves us so vulnerable," she whispered.

"And brings us such joy. I can't tell you how much I love you."

"You really mean it?" she said dazedly.

"You're stuck with me, sweetheart."

"Forever?"

"And a day."

The look in his eyes dazzled Kelsey with happiness. "You don't know how I've longed to hear you say those words! Luke, we're so lucky, us and the baby."

"I swear I'll do my best—for you and for our child. Or, who knows? Children."

"Two," she said. "A boy and a girl would be nice."

He traced the line of her cheekbone with one finger. "I've learned something else too. Home is wherever we're together."

"So the penthouse will really become our home?"

"Ruby-red towels and all. Don't you see, Kelsey? You've brought all the colors of the rainbow into my life."

"Towels, placemats and carpets," she said, with a smile of such tenderness that his throat clogged with emotion.

He said roughly, "I'm sorry it's taken me this long—that I've caused you so much pain."

She stood on tiptoes and kissed him on the mouth. "You're forgiven."

"On our wedding day I promised to love you, remember?"

"To love and to cherish," she said softly.

"It's a promise I'll always keep," Luke said.

No more broken promises, and Kelsey at his side for the rest of his life. Had there ever been a man happier than he was right now? Luke leaned down to kiss her, knowing he held the whole world in his arms.

Knowing he'd come home.

REQUEST YOUR FREE BOOKS!

HARLEQUIN *Presents*

PASSION · SEDUCTION · GUARANTEED

2 FREE NOVELS
PLUS 2
FREE GIFTS!

YES! Please send me 2 FREE Harlequin Presents® novels and my 2 FREE gifts. After receiving them, if I don't wish to receive any more books, I can return the shipping statement marked "cancel." If I don't cancel, I will receive 6 brand-new novels every month and be billed just $3.80 per book in the U.S., or $4.47 per book in Canada, plus 25¢ shipping and handling per book and applicable taxes, if any*. That's a savings of close to 15% off the cover price! I understand that accepting the 2 free books and gifts places me under no obligation to buy anything. I can always return a shipment and cancel at any time. Even if I never buy another book from Harlequin, the two free books and gifts are mine to keep forever.

106 HDN EEXK 306 HDN EEXV

Name	(PLEASE PRINT)	
Address		Apt. #
City	State/Prov.	Zip/Postal Code

Signature (if under 18, a parent or guardian must sign)

Mail to the **Harlequin Reader Service®:**
IN U.S.A.: P.O. Box 1867, Buffalo, NY 14240-1867
IN CANADA: P.O. Box 609, Fort Erie, Ontario L2A 5X3

Not valid to current Harlequin Presents subscribers.

Want to try two free books from another line?
Call 1-800-873-8635 or visit www.morefreebooks.com.

* Terms and prices subject to change without notice. NY residents add applicable sales tax. Canadian residents will be charged applicable provincial taxes and GST. This offer is limited to one order per household. All orders subject to approval. Credit or debit balances in a customer's account(s) may be offset by any other outstanding balance owed by or to the customer. Please allow 4 to 6 weeks for delivery.

Your Privacy: Harlequin is committed to protecting your privacy. Our Privacy Policy is available online at www.eHarlequin.com or upon request from the Reader Service. From time to time we make our lists of customers available to reputable firms who may have a product or service of interest to you. If you would prefer we not share your name and address, please check here. ☐

HP07

HARLEQUIN *Presents*

We've captured a royal slice of life
in our miniseries

By Royal Command

KINGS, COUNTS, DUKES AND PRINCES...

Don't miss these stories of charismatic kings,
commanding counts, demanding dukes and
playboy princes. Read all about their privileged
lives, love affairs...even their scandals!

Let us treat you like a queen—
relax and enjoy our regal miniseries.

Lizzy Mitchell has something Prince Rico Ceraldi
wants: she's the adoptive mother of the heir to his
throne! Lizzy will do anything to keep her son—and
then Rico demands a marriage of convenience....

ROYALLY BEDDED, REGALLY WEDDED

by Julia James

Book #2611, On sale March 2007